3 Tales of Horror

PHASE 5
PHASE 5 PUBLISHING, LLC
PO BOX 1595
ASHEVILLE, NC 28802
WWW.PHASE5PUBLISHING.COM

Horror, fantasy, science fiction. Super-villain, espionage, spy, apocalypse, religion, cults, aliens, mutation, vampires, things which man was not meant to know, occult, other dimensions, forbidden knowledge, reality manipulation, supernatural, evil object

Adult readers: violence; brief, mildly-graphic sexual situations; frequent cursing; death; mutation; death of children; evil object; addiction; suggested insanity; mental manipulation; death of animals and creatures.

Phase 5 Elements: Forbidden Knowledge 111 (Kf111); Super-villain 301 (Sv301); Transmutation 195 (Tm195)

ISBN 978-1-942342-78-6; Printed and Distributed by Lightning Source, a member of the Ingram Content Group, in the United States of America and worldwide
E-book ISBN 978-1-942342-77-9; Distributed by Lulu through the Ingram Content Group, in the United States of America and worldwide

Table of Contents

The Solution

by Rick McQuiston

Prologue

The newscaster seemed agitated as she addressed the camera. Her curly brown hair was tangled with tree twigs and her mascara was blotted around her eyes, giving her a strange gothic look. Her clothes were dirty and tattered, as if she had been in some scuffle. She had obviously not slept in days, and her exhaustion was clear.

"There have been numerous reports from all over the country concerning people, whom some are describing as a type of vampire, having overrun nearly everything in their path.

"These creatures have been reported in areas ranging from rural farmlands to major metropolitan cities. They have been seen in lands as far north as the Northern Territories of Canada and seem to be spreading without regard for human or animal life. The federal government has issued a state of emergency for…a state of emergency-" her eyes widened and all the blood drained from her face.

Suddenly her head was lopped cleanly off her shoulders. The chalk-white creature standing directly behind her scowled in triumph at his conquest, his grotesque face splattered with blood, sinews straining at his skin, eyes burning like a nightmare as he looked at the camera. He lunged and the camera canted sideways, the screen went dark.

1

Brad pushed the little girl back, shielding her from the flying jagged glass. He knew the windows would not keep them out. He also knew the crucifixes would only have a minimal effect, if any at all. One needed faith for them work, and he could not lie to himself about the strength of his.

Brad grabbed the little girl, tossed her over his shoulder, and darted towards the library at the far end of the hallway. He ignored the bleeding gash in his leg.

The man who lived in the house had obviously believed in the supernatural; the crucifixes and various religious artifacts filling the walls attested strongly to that. Brad could only pray that he had wooden stakes or something, anything that would stop the bloodsucking nightmares that had overrun the country.

Breathing a sigh of relief, Brad slammed the heavy wrought iron door shut behind them, sliding a thick metal bar across and into its slot. He leaned up against the door as if hearing their approach might delay their pursuit somehow. He knew vampires feared wrought iron; clearly the owner of the house did as well.

Brad's mind wondered briefly about the whereabouts of the owner. He was not here, in this sanctuary, perhaps he fled elsewhere. Brad had not noted any signs of blood or bodies anywhere else in the house, so he assumed the man had made it out safely.

The little girl seemed remarkably calm given the dangerous and frightening circumstances, and seated herself behind the large oak desk that dominated the room. Her long black hair reflected the moonlight cascading down from the series of small, round skylights high in the ceiling. It gave her a somewhat mysterious look he found disturbing on one so young.

She said not a word and showed no indication of fear or worry. Hundreds, if not thousands, of vicious, bloodthirsty vampires trying to get to them and not a trace of panic on a girl of no more than six years old. Brad still felt compelled to console her. He had lost his little sister, and in an odd sort of way he felt a connection to this strange little girl.

"Are you okay, honey?" Brad whispered. The air in the room was thick with stagnation. "What's your name?"

The little girl looked up from the desktop. Saying nothing, she peered past Brad's shoulder at the heavy iron door. Her eyes were locked onto it; Brad's words seemed to flutter past her attention like butterflies on a bright, sunny day.

"Honey," Brad asked while trying to keep his expression calm. "Are you hurt? Do you have any injuries?"

Only silence filled the room. Brad's attention followed the little girl's vacant stare over to the door and the incredible carvings covering it. His eyes widened at the plump devils reveling within seething cauldrons, the leering demons feasting upon decayed human body parts, swirling storms punctuated by angry jolts of twisted lightening and dancing imps surrounding screaming victims, prodding them with enormous, bloody pitchforks. Such wicked images, so masterfully etched upon the wrought iron canvas of the door, disturbed him.

Brad took a careful step toward the door and its obscene tableau. He could not explain why it frightened him so deeply, almost as much as the vampires frightened him. Perhaps it was knowing that such a magnificent and equally monstrous door was the only obstacle between them and certain death.

Brad turned his back to horrific masterpiece and stared at the little girl. He wanted to ask her if she knew anything about what was happening, but restrained himself from doing so. He had a nagging suspicion that she knew something, something important, but she *was* only a child, albeit a strange one. Surely she had no idea what was going on. He crept away from the nightmarish door to the front of the desk. He looked into her large eyes and searched for any indication of pain, anything that would help him understand her or their situation.

"Are you okay, honey?" he asked for what felt like the hundredth time. "I know you've seen some pretty scary stuff lately. I sure know I have, and I would guess there's probably more to come, but if we stick together and help each other out, maybe, just maybe, we can figure a way out."

Any hope he had for a response was quickly dashed. The little girl merely continued to stare at the door, their only barrier between life and death.

Frustrated and desperate, Brad threw his arms up in defeat. "Fine. You don't wanna talk, we won't talk. I was just hoping you could tell me something to help us out."

He instantly felt guilty for his outburst. He did not want to frighten the poor little thing any more than she probably already was. But his patience was running out, as was their time. He had other problems to deal with at the moment, such as preparing for when the vampires would find them.

He looked around the room for anything he could

move against the door for added support. The skylights were the only windows in the room, for which Brad was extremely grateful. The walls were covered by thick, sturdy bookshelves, lined from top to bottom with a large variety of tomes of every size and color.

A suspicion entered Brad's mind and refused to fade. Brad walked over to one of the smaller shelves, wedged his fingers behind it as much as he could and pulled.

It moved, but only three or four inches. Brad leaned in as far as he could and peered at the wall. Just as he suspected, it was made of wrought iron.

2

Brad awoke to a headache unlike any he had ever experienced before. He attributed it to the combination of hunger, thirst, exhaustion and fear. His experiences these last few weeks could fill a book. He had lost everyone he had ever cared about and, he feared, more than a small part of himself.

Brad had managed to survive because he was quick and he could think on his feet. He stayed on the move, always watching, never letting himself get cornered. He never left any traces of his whereabouts or clues which might help them track him. Yet the vampires had taken a part of him that could never be replaced, leaving a hole that festered and could never be filled. There was no going back to the way things were before. Even if those terrible creatures simply vanished into thin air, the memories would linger far longer than any man could possibly endure. Insanity would forever be tapping on the fragile barrier of his mind.

Brad looked over at the little girl, who was asleep with her head on the massive desk. Her tiny arms were splayed out on either side of her, and her dirty blond hair obscured most of her face. She reminded Brad of a statue he had once admired in a church.

The sound was small at first, nearly inaudible, but it was there nonetheless.

Scratching.

Light, almost gentle scratching emanating from the other side of the door. It sounded like someone, or some*thing*, was exploring the impediment to its next meal, testing the structure for any weaknesses.

Brad's heart was in his throat. He knew they would be done for if the vampires breached the door and gained access to the room. He knew he had survived so far partially because he always thought one step ahead of the creatures. He anticipated their next move. Now he knew what would happen if he could not find a weapon, or a way to exit the house without being seen.

The vampires' cunning and intelligence were matched only by their savagery. It was as if the greater their numbers, the more strategic and organized they became. Their complex and carefully planned attacks overtook people by the thousands, decimating whole cites, entire countries in a matter of weeks. Different militaries from across the world tried numerous strategies against them, but only succeeded in delaying their own demise. Their training and tactics had simply never even contemplated such an enemy. It became painfully apparent early on that the world just was not prepared to deal with the vampires on any level.

Brad carefully, quietly, crawled over to the door and rested his ear on it. At first he heard nothing more than the scratching noises, but then-

Whispers.

Thin, growling murmurs, barely suppressed, sounded as if they were about to burst out at full volume any moment. Brad backed away from the door. Something in his gut, fostered by his many terrible experiences, warned him not to get too close.

And then all hell broke loose on the other side of the door.

The vampires had sensed, or smelled, someone inside the room and their lust for blood erupted with such terrible intensity that Brad fell backwards onto his rear end in a reflexive move to get away from the noise.

He watched in disbelief as the door was

assaulted so violently it bent inward slightly, straining at the heavy iron hinges. His eyes and mind searched for a way out. Leaning back, he looked over his shoulder at the little girl who was now wide awake and staring at him. His desperation overrode his concern for her.

"You have to tell me if you know anything. Where to find a weapon. Or a way out. Please. Our lives depend on it."

The pandemonium on the other side of the door grew louder. They were fighting with each other to get at the door, smashing their powerful fists into it continuously. With each terrible hit the door bent minutely. With each deformation the iron wailed a metallic cry of pain and resistance. The creatures' assault on the door and each other intensified, creating a chorus of ear-splitting horror. Within a minute huge dents littered the face of it, some looking as if they would rupture with one more hit.

"Please, do you know how to stop this? Can you help me stop this?"

She continued to stare at him, either ignoring or not understanding his words.

"What's your name? Do you live here? Where are your parents?" Brad had to restrain himself from losing his temper again. This was definitely not the time for it, and it would only make matters worse.

Maybe she was in shock. Perhaps she had suffered some injury to the head, or was just born with some type of mental deficiency. She appeared to be in perfect health. No fever, no bruises, no bleeding, nothing.

Brad wondered just how much longer the door would hold. Maybe another hour, maybe only another minute. Either way it did not matter unless he could

find some solution. And then it occurred to him.
What if there isn't one?

3

Brad found himself slipping away from this awful moment. He had survived so much for so long that the idea he might actually be at the end of the line just would not completely register. He began to feel even more helpless than when he first witnessed the vampires' attack. He could never forget the poor teenage girl who was so swiftly dispatched by the creatures. She never even knew what hit her.

So young. So innocent. And to perish in such a violent and bloody manner.

Brad had little in the way of family. His mother had passed away when he was just a toddler, and left him with only his alcoholic father and his little sister, Amy.

Amy. She was so beautiful and smart, and such a pretty name too. Brad had always been very close to her, consoling her when she was down, spending time with her whenever he could, and generally being like a father to her. He felt someone should take care of her, since their real father cared more for his whiskey and vodka than his own kids.

The memory of her death stung Brad like a hot needle, probing with its sharp tip, grinding its point into his very heart and soul.

"Brad, help me," Amy had cried as two vampires dragged her kicking and screaming through her bedroom window. "Braaad!"

Brad ran into her bedroom when he heard her scream, but only got there in time to see his little sister being pulled away to her doom. He had tried before to talk her out of keeping her bed directly underneath her window. He should have made her listen.

Not that it would really have made a difference.

His name was the last word he heard her say.

He thought it poetic that her final word was his name, the person who loved her most, the one who had tried so hard to give her something close to a normal family life.

But I failed her when it really mattered. He felt guilty for not jumping through the window and chasing after her, but the shock and utter helplessness had crippled him completely. He told himself he could not have caught the vampires anyway, they were much too fast. Within a few seconds they had been nearly out of sight. And even if he had caught them, what then?

4

The door was holding up very well, considering the vampires' onslaught. Brad shuddered when he thought of what must be happening on the other side of the door. He had seen their ferocity and power first hand. Even wrought iron did little to deter them, if they were hungry or angry enough. Their need and rage would overcome their fear, eventually they would find a way to get through, indifferent to their own safety.

Brad was surprised when the little girl abruptly stood up from behind the desk and walked over to where he stood. Her eyes conveyed pity as well as a sense of confidence. She seemed oblivious to the thrashing the door was taking from the vampires, and focused directly on Brad.

Now that he had her attention, his desperation insisted he get her to speak. "Do you know what is going on here?"

"My name is…." She paused, seating herself on the floor. "My name is… actually, I am not quite sure what my name is, or if I ever had one at all." A tear welled in her eye. "If I ever had one at all."

Any fear that was crippling Brad's thoughts melted away.

"I know you're probably frightened. I am, but we have to try and find a way out of this mess." He waited for a reaction from her. Nothing. "Listen to me. That door probably won't hold too much longer, not with the way those things are attacking it. If there is anything that you're not telling me, anything at all, please say it. Maybe it can help us somehow."

The little girl wiped her tears away and thought for a moment. "Follow me," she said with a hint of a smile.

Brad eagerly trailed behind her, his hope for

survival reviving slightly.

She sauntered casually over to the enormous oak desk in the center of the room. She reached down, pushed her dark hair out of her face, opened the lower left drawer. Brad resisted crowding her. Apparently she knew exactly what she was looking for. Now that she was doing something, he was not going to hinder her in any way.

She clamped both her tiny hands around a large, faded red book and withdrew it from the drawer. It was at least three inches thick and tightly bound with a heavy iron clasp, like nothing he had ever seen before. All he could determine was that it seemed old and odd. She plopped it down onto the desktop with a heavy thud and looked up at Brad.

"This might be of some help to you," she muttered. "I'm not sure where you need to look, but the answers you seek are contained within it."

Brad noted she had a strange grasp of language for someone so young. "I'll see what I can find," he announced with what little confidence he had left.

"But please hurry," the little girl warned as she glanced over at the door. "We haven't much time."

Now she notices, he thought, then pushed his annoyance aside in favor of finding something— anything—that might give them an edge when the living nightmare breached the door.

Brad picked up the heavy tome and studied the clasp. It was a fairly simple mechanism, possibly unlocked with a key of some sort, and tarnished with streaks of rust. He flipped the book on its side and began to tap on the lock with his finger. Four tiny pinholes appeared out of nowhere, one on each side of the lock, and immediately started to flicker, as if they were fading in and out of existence.

"You must be quick. The openings are only visible for a few seconds, and then no more until another time, another time unknown to all."

Her words confused Brad, but he did not have time to figure her out right now. The vampires were attacking the door with more ferocity than ever, beating on it with their deformed white heads and filthy talons.

Brad felt helpless. What was he supposed to do?

"You'll need this," the little girl said as if reading his thoughts. She held up a small, unusual-looking device with four thin arms protruding from its edges. Brad took it from her and placed it squarely on top of the lock mechanism. The arms instantly clamped down on the book, locking into the four tiny holes. Then a heavy clicking sounded inside and Brad nearly shouted with joy. A few seconds later the device fell off to the side of the book, taking the lock mechanism along with it.

"You must hurry," the little girl reminded Brad. "You must be quick."

Brad flipped open the book and began scouring the delicate, yellowed pages.

5

Brad nearly vomited when he focused his attention on some of the pictures in the book: bloodied body parts, obese zombies rolling in human remains, laughing demons chucking screaming people into huge blazing pits. Brad tried to pass by the worst pages, but still had to at least look over them to some degree. He had no idea what he was searching for and could not afford to miss it, whatever it may be.

He rifled through the pages with the sounds of the voracious monsters smashing into the door ringing in his ears. Hunger was threatening to cripple him, as was thirst and just plain exhaustion, but he could not stop. Not now. He irrationally felt that possibly the future of mankind was involved, and he just might be the last chance. His grumbling and shrinking stomach and dry throat would just have to take a back seat. There were much more important things.

After seventy-five or eighty pages, Brad slammed his fist down in frustration. A drop of blood welled up beneath his palm, staining the desk and inflaming the vampires' attack on the door.

"How am I supposed to know what to look for?" he shouted. "How is a stupid book going to stop those things outside? What am I supposed to do?"

The little girl stared at him in puzzlement. She brushed her hair from her face and sat back down at the desk.

"Don't let your fear overrule your determination. Continue your search. The solution will present itself to you in due time."

He almost longed for her silence again. "We don't have time for this! If you know something you have to tell me now!" Brad felt his emotions getting the better of his logic, and he feared completely losing his temper.

The little girl smiled at him. "I know you feel lost, but you must persevere. The fate of mankind might depend on it."

Girded by her validation of his desperate hope, Brad resumed looking through the pages of the book, hoping and praying he could find some useful information before it was too late. He concentrated as best as he could, trying to block out the terrible noise coming from behind the door. He began to babble while he flipped through the pages, struggled to maintain his composure, his sanity.

"Paaaage two-hundred forty-sevennnn," a gravelly voice screeched, the tone of a dentist's drill, high-pitched and full of promises of pain.

Brad's head snapped up from the book. His heart fell in his chest and the blood in his veins froze solid. Fear like he had never known gripped his mind.

The voice had come from the other side of the door.

6

The vampires were collecting in vast numbers. They roamed the countryside in packs of thousands, searching in an endless journey for food, death and destruction. For countless centuries they had waited, endured endless hardships and the suffering of their twisted, soulless bodies, frequently attempting to escape from their plight, always meeting with failure and pain. The phenomena that allowed their escape from their native plane was not understood, only exploited.

They did learn something from their near-endless torment: patience.

Patience allowed them to gather around the house where Brad and the little girl were hiding. It allowed them to study the building, its defenses and structural weaknesses. It allowed them to plan their attack and wait for just the right time to strike.

Despite all reason and caution, Brad felt compelled to listen to the voice and turn to page two-forty-seven of the book. The pages grew warmer as he flipped through them. He dismissed the observation as soon as it registered. *Just the exhaustion.*

Page two-forty-seven bore writing that was nearly illegible. The words were scrawled in thick black ink with swirls of bright red mingled freely throughout the text. Brad strained to decipher the writing, but only succeeded in frustrating himself further. It was apparently in some ancient language.

"I can't read this! This is hopeless." The notion of fighting his way past the vampires began to appear like an attractive alternative. This book, that door, this girl, that noise, it was just too much. He had fought them before and survived, he could do it again.

The little girl calmly stood and walked around the desk to where Brad stood. She grasped his hand, squeezed tightly, pulled it over to the open pages in the book.

"Feel your pain," she whispered to him. "Know the aches in your heart and use them as a portal to better things, to solutions for problems."

Brad felt anger rising up in his gut. "What does that mean?" he shouted at her. "Talk normal, not in riddles. We don't have time for games."

Her calm demeanor did not falter. "Use the anger and remorse you've experienced as a key. Only then will you be able to unlock doors and remove barricades."

Brad looked at her as a single tear rolled down his face. Maybe it was the exhaustion, but suddenly her strange words were beginning to make sense to him. "You mean use the pain in my life…as a weapon?"

The little girl smiled. "If that is how you interpret it, then yes."

"But how?" Brad almost whined.

"The book is a tome of pain. Only those who have experienced pain in its purest form can truly decipher its meaning."

"Amy," Brad choked. "I lost my sister, who I loved dearly. Those things took her, and my father. I want revenge. I need it to complete me. Even if we get out of this mess, without it I would feel empty."

"Good," the little girl encouraged. "Good."

"But whose voice was that out there, who told me the page number to turn to?"

The little girl's smile suddenly vanished. "My father."

For just a second Brad forgot about the vampires in the hallway. His heart reached out to the little girl, feeling her loss and relating to it completely.

"Who was your father?"

The little girl smiled again. Her face brightened like a child on Christmas morning. "His name is Dr. Artimus Vinheiser. He is a prominent archeologist and a revered collector of ancient and historically important artifacts."

"I've heard of him before. I think I've seen him on TV before."

The little girl nodded. "He discovered the book while on one of his many expeditions to Northern Europe."

Her attention was suddenly diverted to the door. The top left corner of it was being bent inward, filling the room with a terrible noise. A single, pure white skeletal hand emerged from the opening, wavered in the air for a moment or two, clenched into a tight, angry fist. A thin trickle of bone-colored dust drifted down to the floor from it.

Brad turned around and bit his lip. The blood had drained from his face when he saw the clawed hand, a painting of impending death situated directly behind him, but he somehow pushed it out of his mind and focused on what the little girl was telling him.

"We have to hurry," he cried. "Tell me, what did your father do?"

The little girl looked back into his eyes. "My father found the book and purchased it from a rare books dealer; he was anxious to add it to his collection, to uncover whatever secrets it held within its pages. He brought it home and started to delve into its mysteries, but was soon sidetracked by his other work. For months the book sat gathering dust and cobwebs, forgotten. It shared wall space with hundreds of other volumes, biding its time, and waiting." She looked over Brad's shoulder again at the door, a slight trace of fear etched on her face. "The book would not be denied, however, and eventually tapped into my father's mind to extract whatever pain it could."

Brad could hardly believe what he was hearing. He shook his head as if to rearrange the information. "The book extracted his pain?"

"It tried to, but found there was virtually none to take. Dr. Artimus Vinheiser had led a completely enviable life, void of pain or misfortune. His family always had wealth, and his health was robust."

The skeletal hand was soon joined by others. Within a few minutes there were at least ten of them, all thrashing back and forth, smashing into each other in vicious attempts to gain access to the room. Slimy black residue dripped down the grotesquely decorated surface of the door from several of the hands, coating it in a ghastly layer of stench and decay. The smell was becoming unbearable. He was suddenly glad his stomach was so empty.

He was sweating so much he could hardly keep his face dry. His head hurt and he felt his heart thumping wildly in his chest. The fact that he might not be able to take too much more weighed heavily on his weary and frightened mind. "Then what did the book do?" he asked, not really believing he was having this conversation or wanting to hear the answer.

The little girl sighed. "My father did have one great joy in his life. His work fulfilled him, but not completely. It nourished him, but only to the point that material accomplishments could. His wife was what really sustained him, kept him striving to be a better man, for her and for himself."

Brad found himself mesmerized by the little girl's words, but knew he did not have the luxury of listening to her complete story. Time was running out.

"Please, we have to hurry", he reminded her. "Those things are getting-"

The face peering at him through the small breach in the door froze his words in his mouth. The vampire stared at him with such hatred and evil that the expression alone was nearly enough to stop Brad's heart.

"And then it happened," the little girl added in a somber tone, oblivious to the malevolent creature glaring at them from the doorway. "The day came like a lightening bolt, jarring my father loose from the comfort of his daily life, and sending him into deep despair."

"What happened?"

"His wife died and the book took advantage of his pain."

9

Questions swirled in Brad's mind like an insect swarm, but there, at the heart of them all, was one.

Why?

He reached for the core of his anger, found a memory.

"Brad, why don't ya go on an' help your little sister some. I don't feel like it right now," his father slurred. Brad could smell the whiskey on his breath and could see the irresponsible laziness in his bloodshot eyes. He would rather be drinking than taking care of his own daughter. "Go on, son, get going, ya hear me?" The words stung like a thousand needles.

Brad had learned to turn his anger with his father into a useful tool, a reminder to himself to be a better man, to try harder, to never give up. His father had stopped caring about anything when his wife had died, even his own children.

"Noooo!" Brad cried at the top of his lungs, releasing all the pent up rage and torment he had endured. The outburst was so sudden and salient that even the vampires paused in their assault on the door. After a few seconds they resumed their efforts, seemingly nourished by the anguish of their prey.

Brad struggled to maintain his composure. "I've tried my whole life to be strong, to never give up, but I feel like I'm nearing the end of my rope. I honestly don't know how much longer I can hold out."

The little girl smiled at him, wrapping him up in her warmth and confidence. "Use your pain. Defy the book as it tries to feed off of it."

Brad continued. "I've never had a true father

figure, or a mother, either. I've always felt as if I was on my own. "

"Yes, continue. I understand."

"My life has been one thing after another, one problem leading into the next. My father was only a part of it, a big part granted, but still just a part of it." Brad noticed the book sitting on the desk behind him. There was a very faint greenish glow around it, which seemed to originate from beneath it, and spread out like cigarette smoke. It pulsed with movement, with some type of life. "I want this all to end! I'm sick of it! Sick of those filthy vampires, and sick of this stinking house!"

The book swelled, releasing a thick odor similar to rancid meat, but even more overpowering. It practically coated the room, leaving no corner untainted, staining everything with its corrupt stench.

The little girl noticed the book as well. Her eyes were fastened to it. Her thoughts racing with its movements. She knew what it was capable of, what it would do if it were able to.

"Now," she instructed Brad. "Twist your pain to your own will. Use it as a weapon, not a deterrent to your goals and desires. The book will sense this and release its bonds on my father… hopefully."

Brad only partly understood what she was saying, but did as she said regardless. He flung his head back and gripped his painful memories and frustrations by the roots, swinging them around like a whip, twisting them to his desires, utilizing them to his own advantage. The memory of watching his father being yanked to his death by a vampire the size of a large gorilla, with a face to match, the only time Brad was actually glad that his father had drank himself into oblivion.

The memory of running to Mrs. Honner's house, seeking the solace and safety of her kindness.

Just as he arrived on her front porch her body was catapulted through the front bay window. Her head had been torn clean off and a short, half-decayed vampire squatted in her front room, munching on what was left of her face. The thing glared at him with such evil hunger and hatred that Brad's stomach expelled the remainder of his last meal onto the porch. The creature tossed her half-eaten head aside and bounded through the air straight for him, fangs gnashing, blood coating its stained and tattered shirt. The howl and throes of the creature after Brad impaled it with a spindle ripped from the porch frame. The fetid pile of pitch-black ash laced with an underlying putrid slime that marked the end of the vile monster.
And for the first time in his life, he actually felt like a true, red-blooded hero.

The vampires in the hallway wailed at the top of their dry-rotted lungs in frustration. Hundreds of the unnatural fiends howled and hissed, increasing their assault on the door. Above all the noise, on the other side of the door Brad heard Dr. Artimus Vinheiser. He was shouting and laughing cheers of relief, his jubilation rivaling the vampires' horrible screeching. Brad could hear him smashing against them, thrashing them within an inch of oblivion. Beating them to a powdery pulp. Doing what he could to end their terrible reign.
And then in a swift second, all was silent.
Both Brad and the little girl cautiously walked over to the door and pressed their ears to it, avoiding

the trails of black ichor, holding their breath. The stillness was deafening and seemed to last for hours. Brad looked over at the little girl and smiled, and she smiled back at him. And then a single phrase filtered through the silence and into the room. It was simple, but its meaning was clear and powerful. The words cut through the hopelessness that had filled the library, offering promises of real hope that Brad had not felt in a long time.

"Thank you."

It had not been long since Brad had settled down to get some rest. The sleep he had managed to steal was troubled and sparse at best, but it was enough to sustain him and replenish his energy. He rubbed his swollen eyes and ran his fingers through his disheveled hair, noted it seemed to be thinning. Hunger and thirst competed for his attention, but he pushed them from his thoughts as best he could. They were the least of his worries.

"Hello. I hope you slept well enough. I was tempted to wake you, but thought better of it. You needed rest to regain your strength."

Brad sat up and stretched his aching limbs to the point of straining. "Good morning to you, too," he replied. His head felt like it had been run over by a truck, but overall he felt as if he would be able to get through the day. "How long was I out for?" he asked between yawns.

The little girl pushed the hair out of her face. "Approximately two hours, perhaps more."

"Boy, did I ever need that. Have there been any signs of those things?" Brad held on to a slight bit of hope that the vampires were gone, but resisted getting his hopes up too high. Experience had taught him to expect the worst.

"Absolutely nothing. Only the occasional squeaks and moans from an old house such as this one." Her expression did not reflect the ordeal she had been through. It was cheerful, full of promise and hope, and wholly unstained by recent events.

"Are you sure you're all right?" Brad asked. "I'm pretty sure I can find some first aid if you need any."

The little girl shook her head. "No, thank you," she politely replied. "I feel quite well."

Her attention quickly swung back to the door. Brad followed her eyes and realized that she must have been thinking of her father. He truly felt bad for her, but he remained reluctant to open the door. His instincts told him it still might be dangerous.

"I know you would like to see your father again," he said. "But until I'm a hundred percent sure it's safe out there I'm not going to open that door. Do you understand?"

The little girl looked up at him, her eyes watering. "I understand you perfectly," she answered. "I accepted a long time ago that my father would never return to me. I knew in my heart that I would never see his smile again, or hear his laugh, or feel his love. All these things I grew to acknowledge, despite the pain of doing so. But the mere thought 'the only barrier between him and I is that door' is almost too much to resist. I feel compelled to at least see if he is there, and if so, if he is all right."

Brad had a hard time arguing with her logic, especially since it was fairly obvious the vampires had gone. And sooner or later they would need to leave the room and find some food and water.

"Okay, fine," he finally conceded. "But I'm only opening it a few inches, just enough to see what's out there. Understand?" He hated to be so stern with her, especially after what they had been through, but at this point fear governed his actions, for better or worse.

The little girl nodded and promptly stood. She walked over to the door and rested her small hands on it. Brad watched her for a tense moment or two before walking up behind her and gently pushing her aside.

"All right then," he whispered nervously. "I hope

we don't regret doing this."

"All will be well," the little girl replied with an innocent smile. "I know it will."

With effort tempered by reluctance Brad slid the heavy iron bar back and twisted the doorknob slightly. Fear laced his thoughts as he peered through the thin opening, squinting, hoping to God that there was nothing there.

The little girl hopped up and down behind Brad as she attempted to see through the opening. For the first time she was acting like a child her age. "Can you see anything?" she whispered anxiously. "Is there anyone there?"

Brad ignored her. His main concern was for their safety, not her curiosity or her desire to see her father.

"Take it easy," he said as he tried to look down the hallway through the thin crack in the doorway. "I'm trying to see if there's anyone there."

He scanned back and forth as best as he could, but the lighting in the hallway was not very good. Only sporadic beams of pale moonlight filtered into the passage, sporadically illuminating empty corners and sparse, dusty walls loosely decorated with forgotten relics and pictures. The floor revealed only traces of the creatures' remains; a few distorted footprints scattered about in sooty black residual ash, and some rotted pieces of cloth that seemed very old, somehow perverse in design.

Brad exhaled deeply as he felt a world of worry slide off his shoulders. For the first time in ages he felt as if there might actually be hope for the future of mankind, and for himself. He had been at war with his own guilt for as long as he had with the vampires.

The little girl was practically jumping up and down. "Is my father there? Is my father there?" she continually asked. "Do you see him? Is he there?"

Brad hated to disappoint her. "I'm sorry honey," he solemnly said. "But I don't see anything except for some ashes and a few pieces of old clothing. Your father must have succeeded. I think he destroyed them."

Against his better judgment Brad began to open

the door a little more. He was very cautious, but still felt vulnerable. The realization that he needed some type of weapon struck him suddenly, and he looked back into the room to see if there was anything he could use.

He quickly walked over to the desk and tore off a piece of wood from one of the drawers. It was crude, but sharp, and would probably be effective if he needed it.

The book sat on the edge of the desk, its power undiminished. Brad felt it tap into his thoughts, compeling him to open it, to delve into its terrible secrets once again.

Brad felt the evil pull from the book, but pushed it aside fairly easily. Strange and perverse as its influence was, he had locked down his emotions the night Amy died. He would make sure that he was the one in control. With a quick jab he pushed the book off the edge of the desk, causing it to land with a heavy thud on the dusty floor. It sunk almost an inch as soon as it landed, leaving a deep impression in the metal as small dust clouds settled back on the floor.

Brad swung back around and strutted toward the open doorway where the little girl stood waiting for him. "Follow me," he instructed. "And above all, stay close."

The hallway loomed before them like a cold, dark tunnel. It radiated a strange type of aura, similar to a long forgotten prison, deserted but still powerful in its desolation, still haunted by the evil deeds of its former occupants. Brad was sure he still heard faint echoes of the creaking and screeching the deformed door had made as he had slowly pushed it open, as if they were in a deep cavern instead of a house.

"Stay close," Brad reminded the little girl. "We don't know anything for sure. Just because it looks safe doesn't mean it is." His mind flashed back to Mrs. Honner's brutal demise.

The little girl clung to his shirt. She held on both out of fear and from her desire to follow his instructions. She knew that even if she found her father he probably would not, or could not, help them much, if at all. In a lot of ways they were on their own.

"I will," she promised with a small nod, and positioned herself as close to Brad as she could.

Thin rays of moonlight streamed into the hallway from three small overhead skylights, mainly, but only slightly, due to the increasing cloud cover outside. It seemed as if the corridor was a mile long with no promise of safety or security at the end of it. All it offered was a path.

The first few steps into the hallway were some of the most difficult Brad had ever taken in his life. He felt as if he were a toddler who was just learning to walk, stumbling and ready to latch onto any nearby table or chair for support. Only this time his life was at stake.

"Stay close to me," he repeated, more for himself than for the little girl. "No matter what happens, stay close." His experiences had him entertaining the horrible, but very real, possibility of something happening to her. Just the thought of it sent an ice-cold shiver down his spine. He vowed to himself that he would die before he let anything happen to the nameless little girl.

They carefully moved forward, waiting a few seconds between each step to make sure there were no consequences. Dangers could be lurking around every corner, within every shadow, inside every unseen area. There was no real way to be sure except to move forward, survey the situation and move forward again. However, they might not have much time, so being overly cautious was not a luxury they could really afford, either.

Brad picked up his pace slightly and the little girl followed close behind him. The vampires could attack at any moment, a fact not lost on him, and he felt that getting out of the house might be their best chance for survival. What had once promised a sanctuary now felt like a prison. *Or worse.*

"Let me know if you see any signs of my father," the little girl whispered. "Please, I need to know whether he is still alive."

"Don't worry honey," Brad replied without taking his eyes off his surroundings. "I'll let you know."

The little girl smiled nervously. "Thank you very much. I mean it."

Brad smiled as well but still kept his eyes on the hallway ahead of them. "Don't mention it," he said. "Don't mention it at all."

The sound was small at first, escalating gradually until it reached a level impossible to ignore. It faintly resembled sharp nails gliding across a chalkboard, but far more unnerving. Apparently, something was trying to get into the house.

Brad froze where he stood, the little girl bumped into him.

"What is that sound?" she asked breathlessly. "Where is it coming from?"

Brad's eyes narrowed. "I'm not sure, but I think it's from around the corner, possibly near the front doorway. We'll have to pass by there if we want to get out of here. I don't think there's any way of avoiding it."

He tried to suppress a thought that fluttered into his weary mind, but failed and it took root there. *What if whatever's outside the house making those noises is not trying to get in, at least not yet, anyway? Suppose it's trying to gain access, not to the house, but to my mind? Toying with its prey in a demented game of cat and mouse.* Brad shuddered, chided himself for letting his imagination go there, but continued to creep forward.

The hallway ended approximately fifteen feet ahead, where it branched off to the left, which led directly to the front door, and to the right, which led to one of the main living rooms. A huge crystal chandelier hung over the front foyer and another near the entranceway to the living room. Neither of them provided any light. The only illumination was from thin beams of faint moonlight cascading in through the cracks in the front door frame.

Brad flicked the light switches as he came across them, but they yielded only empty clicks.

"There's no power in the whole house," he moaned in dismay. "Those filthy things must have torn down the lines or something." *Or they've destroyed the power station.* He took a deep breath and tried to steady his frayed nerves. "We'll have to try to find some candles or a flashlight."

The little girl nodded and continued staring ahead. The noises were subsiding a little.

"I don't think we'll be able to make it out the front door," Brad whispered. "Whatever is making those noises... the sound seems to be coming from there, more or less. It might be right outside the house waiting for us. I think we'll stand a better chance if we try to go through the house, even find another way out besides the back door." He watched her expression to see if she disagreed, if she had anything to add.

The little girl nodded in agreement and gripped Brad's hand tightly. "If you say so," she whispered. "But I'm not exactly sure of the best way to go. Most of the time I have lived here my father was hesitant to leave too many lights on. He said it hurt his eyes and clouded his judgment. This house has always stood in shadows. Always. Like shadows are part of this building."

"You mean to tell me you have no idea how this place is laid out, or where the back door is?" Brad tried to control his irritation, but his grip on his temper was wearing thin again.

The little girl nodded. "I'm afraid not."

Brad clenched his jaw and pulled her along behind him. "Fine, then, I'll just have to find a way out of this place on my own."

Every step Brad and the little girl took felt like a mile. Shadows hung in every corner like jet-black lions waiting to pounce on prey. He felt as if they were going around in circles. The house was in some way distorted, unnatural in its design. Walls came out of nowhere and met at tilted angles, impossibly holding up heavy ceilings and fixtures. Dark shadows sprawled across large areas unbroken. Floors sunk toward one side, but met with neighboring walls at higher spots, defying the laws of physics and common sense.

Brad rubbed his aching head and swollen eyes. He felt as if they were in a funhouse, although this place was far more sinister. Vampires could still be lurking inside it, and a heavy sense of dread hung in the stagnant air, choking whatever hope remained.

His mind touched on memories of the neighborhood carnivals of his childhood. The aura surrounding all of the rides and booths was both frightening and intoxicating. But back then he was able to rely on his youth and exuberance to overcome all the unsettling aspects associated with carnivals and their workforce. And most important of all, he was able to go home afterward, and leave the weirdness behind. This dark funhouse offered no such securities or promises. There were no safe places anymore, and he was certain now that this house was farther from safe than most.

"I think the kitchen area is through that way," the little girl whispered, pointing toward another long hallway. "I can't be entirely sure, though."

Brad looked down at her. He did not want to trust their lives to a strange child who did not know her way around her own home, but was desperate enough to consider it. He was beginning to doubt his own judgment, and the possibility that the little girl just might be right prompted him to follow her suggestion.

"All right," he said hesitantly. "If you feel that is the way to go, we'll try it. I guess as long as we're heading away from those noises...." A light smile creased his face, and he looked at her to try reassure them both. *I hope you're right, though.*

The corridor led from the cavernous family room down into another long, strangely designed passage. It, too, felt unnatural, almost to the point of being cartoonish, as if rendered in an animated setting. Brad hesitated before walking down the hallway, clenching the piece of wood from the desk so tightly his hand ached.

The walls, in keeping with the general theme of the rest of the house, were adorned with more antiquities. Brad wished Dr. Vinheiser had decorated with a lighter, more cheerful theme. *Anything would have been better than "ancient creepy."*

"Stay close," Brad reminded the little girl. "Remember, we're still not sure where we are going in this crazy place."

The little girl nodded. "It is odd," she tilted her head and noted with her gaze a couple of the walls. Her voice remained calm and steady, "My memory of this house is vague at best, but I do not recall the strange architectural designs here before."

Brad immediately froze. "What do you mean?"

"I am not sure this house was constructed this way. Perhaps the situation has altered it somehow."

Brad felt his empty stomach churn. He believed he had seen all the horror the world had to offer: Vampires, loved ones killed literally right before his eyes, strange little girls who seemed to be from another world. But now, houses which had been altered into some weird mockery of common sense? It pushed on his mind that such a thing might be possible, but more so that his strange little hostess could propose such a possibility.

She doesn't even know her own name, or where her kitchen is. And I'm looking to her for help.

His hope for escape from the house withered. He felt insanity tapping on the walls of his mind, trying to gain entry into his psyche.

14

Dr. Artimus Vinheiser stumbled through the room, unsure of where he was or how he had gotten there. The dim glow from the moonlight streaming through several small skylights strained his eyes and caused his head to ache, but he pressed on. Fearing the worst, the price of his past deeds weighed heavily on his soul as well as his body. Bruises covered his torso and arms and blood trickled from numerous lacerations across his exhausted body. All he wanted to do was find his daughter; she was the only thing that mattered now. He knew, felt, she was nearby. And even now, especially now, he trusted his instincts without question.

Horrible memories roamed across his weary mind. Thoughts of the birth of his daughter and the corrupt temptations he had succumbed to thereafter. He had meant well, he constantly reminded himself, but history would not be so kind in its evaluation of him, of that he was certain. *Assuming there would be anyone left to read about it.*

The walls seemed to impede his every step, lashing out in inanimate attempts to thwart his progress. The ceiling dangled overhead, swaying back and forth as if in a twisted dream, threatening to crash down on his head at any moment. He pushed on, energized by his desire to find his only child and fulfill his destiny.

His blurred vision made it difficult to focus on what lay before him, but he was just able to see the outline of where he was. He knew the house well, at least he had before it started to warp, and even though the stench of the fiends still lingered in its darkened rooms, his mind was clear enough to navigate through it. With some help he had managed to destroy the vampires who had forced their way into the house, but he was still unsure of just how many remained outside. Hundreds, he feared, perhaps more.

He did not see the large painting as it materialized out of thin air, manifesting directly in front of his face. He smashed into it head first and crashed to the ground. Lying on his back, trying to focus on the illusive ceiling through dust clogging his senses, the heavy brass-framed painting fell on top of him. It covered his body almost completely, from head to toe, like a blanket, molding itself to the contours of his body.

His weary bloodshot eyes finally focused on the face of death painted on the enormous canvas looming just in front of his nose, threatening to suffocate him. He saw the swirling chaos of black and purple skies and twisting storms entwining the fearsome landscape with jagged bolts of razor-sharp lightening. He saw snarled gaping maws sprouting up out of the rugged ground, sporting infinite rows of gnashing bloodied teeth, grinding up and down as if chewing invisible bodies to gory pulps. He saw the house in the background, his house, the house he was now trapped inside, and he saw himself near the front porch of that same house, bent over at impossible angles, a caricature of his former self, a twisted imitation of his humanity. He was straddling something, someone, at his feet, leering with an expression of hate-filled hunger and power-mad domination. He was towering over the prone figure as if he were master, judge and jury. Even god.

Dr. Vinheiser closed his eyes and welcomed unconsciousness, allowed himself to fall into the welcome darkness of sleep. On some level he felt it might be his only alternative, his only escape from the nightmare that plagued his every waking moment. And he knew he would see his daughter again in his dreams.

15

Brad heard the noise from the other side of the house, as did the little girl. They looked at each other with expressions of worry and hope. Maybe there was another person in the house, someone who needed help, or could help them find a way out.

"We should follow the noise. Maybe it leads to a way out." Brad feared that it was another vampire, but something inside his mind assured him it was not.

They started to make their way toward the sound of the crash. The darkness still obstructed their path and they had to feel their way along more than ever. The walls felt cold and damp, the drywall sinking in slightly with every touch of their hands, crumbling beneath the soggy wallpaper. Brad and the little girl continued to move forward, unsure of where exactly they were going. They knew very well that they could not turn back.

"Can you see anything yet?" the little girl asked quietly.

"No, nothing yet," Brad replied.

He found himself wondering about the book back in the library. Was it really as powerful as she had said? And did it still pose a threat to them? He was not sure, but forced himself to block out any thoughts of it and focus on navigating through the house that seemed to be rotting, or melting, around them. At least the floor seemed solid enough, though it had become more uneven as they made their way to the elusive kitchen.

When Brad and the little girl reached the room from which they were sure the noise had come, they found a large space, dominated by ancient-looking relics and various odds and ends, the sort of stuff a collector would display. And laying in the opposite doorway was an enormous painting, which seemed to be covering something lumpy and roughly the size of a person. Both were completely still.

They bolted over to the painting. Brad quickly pulled the heavy painting aside, and cleared loose debris from a man's face. He was an aged man, possibly in his seventies, and sported a thin white-gray mustache and neatly-trimmed pointed beard. His face was lined with wrinkles and bore the weathering of many years of exploration. But he was nonetheless a handsome man, whose broad build and tasteful attire attested to good breeding and education. It appeared he was a gentleman who took care of himself.

"Is this your father?" Brad asked the little girl.

She knelt at the injured man's side and grasped his hand in hers. "Yes," she whispered. "He is my father."

Artimus Vinheiser opened his eyes and gazed into the face of his daughter.

Despite his condition he recognized her instantly, a slight, painful smile creasing his weathered face.

"I recognize you my child," he said softly. "You have no idea just how long I have been searching for you." He began to cough uncontrollably, but regained his composure as best he could. "I never thought I would see you again."

"You've been looking for her?" Brad asked incredulously. "I thought you left her here, in this house. I…I thought…."

Dr. Vinheiser shook his head slightly, groaned from the discomfort. The heavy canvas had succeeded in compounding his injuries, which were already critical. "No, sir, I did not leave her in this wretched house, at least not by my own choice. I was separated from her by force, a force far greater than any other on this weary planet. A force capable of evil and power beyond the scope of any mere mortal. Something which I could not control, nor even resist."

Brad's look of concern and confusion instantly vanished and was replaced by one of resignation and fear. "The book. It's the book isn't it?"

"Yes, it is the book. *The Tome of Pain*, as it is known in its own plane, in its own world."

The little girl was fighting back tears. Her tangled loose hair hung in front of her dirty face, and her tiny hands shook uncontrollably. It had been so long since she had seen her father; she did not know what to say. All she could do was simply hold his hand and listen to him.

"The book created pain within my life and nourished itself from it," Dr. Vinheiser continued. "It enveloped my soul within its pages, draining whatever happiness there was, growing stronger as it did so."

"But couldn't you have realized what it was and try and stop it, or throw it away, or burn it, anything?"

Dr. Vinheiser sighed. "Can an alcoholic put down the bottle? Can a drug addict throw away the needle? You don't understand and probably never will, but the book had a hold on my will far beyond any control I still possessed. I could destroy it no more than a mother could her own child."

Brad had heard enough. He abruptly stood up and brushed himself off. "For your information sir," he retorted. "I have been acquainted more or less with the book. Just ask your own daughter here." He motioned towards the little girl. "She saw me defeat the book. She saw me manage to overcome it. What do you think destroyed those vampires outside your library? I did. And I am not a particularly strong person. But I still did it. If I could do it, you could have, too."

Instantly Brad felt a pang of guilt and regret for raising his voice like he did, especially in front of the little girl, but did not apologize. All he wanted to do was find a way out of the house. If he could help the little girl as well, then so much the better, but she had her father with her now, and she was no longer his responsibility.

"We need to get out of here now," he announced. "How do we find the back door out of this place?"

Dr. Vinhesier laughed, coughing up droplets of blood in the process. "My dear boy," he croaked. "There isn't a rear door anymore. The house is being twisted by the book to prevent us from leaving. It is probably still hungry and needs to feed again." He weakly lifted his hand and loosened his collar. "I'm sure you have noticed that things around here lately have been a little, shall we say, distorted. It's the book, bending things to its own desires, weaving another truth, another reality, one where those unnatural creatures and desolation rule the Earth. It searched for suitable carriers of its evil, and it eventually found them."

Brad's control of himself slipped some. He was tired of the Vinheisers, tired of the book and this twisted house, tired of all their nonsense. "Listen, I just want to get out of this crazy place. I want no part of demonic books or vampires or little girls and their long lost fathers." Brad breathed, as deeply as his constricted chest would allow, and continued through clenched teeth, "I just want out of here and the best way to do that is to find the back door."

The little girl looked up at Brad with watery eyes.

"I'm sorry that I said that," Brad apologized to her. "But I've managed to get through an awful lot by myself, and I think we'd all be better off on our own from now on." He felt his temper running away with him, but saw no reason to rein it in.

"And what then? What will you do after you've escaped from this house? Surely you are aware that there are many more of those creatures roaming about, possibly right outside the doors of this very building. You must realize that wherever you go, no matter how far away from here it is, that you will never be able to escape from the vampires, or the book, or worse, from yourself." Dr. Vinheiser's voice became strained, and another wave of pain nearly overtook him.

"What is that supposed to mean?" Brad cried. "And how do you know about all this?" He raised an eyebrow at the injured man.

Dr. Vinheiser closed his eyes and forced himself to sit up slightly. He had several broken ribs, and bruises over most of his body, but still managed to suppress his discomfort enough to look Brad in the eyes. "Unfortunately, I'm afraid I had something to do with it."

16

The night air was growing cooler. Thin plumes of gray mist gently wrapped around every leafless tree limb and bush. Off in the distance a lone coyote howled to the pale, full moon, raising its conical snout high above the cold, barren ground as it spewed its night-song into the wastelands.

The vampires crouched low to the once-fertile ground. Their numbers had increased many times over, allowing them to disperse themselves into legions capable of overpowering small villages, or even cities. The larger and more aggressive of their kind led the smaller, less dominant ones by sheer brute force and cruelty. Cannibalism was not uncommon within their ranks, and what one did, the others more or less followed without question.

An enormous, seven-and-a-half foot tall vampire scowled when it caught sight of the large house looming far in the distance. Gifted with excellent eyesight, it could see for miles. It sensed the beings within the building were humans, possibly many of them, and it also sensed something else there as well. Its cold, clammy hands clenched in anger, a jet-black drop of ichor trickled down to the soil. It raised its sinewy arms high into the night sky and wailed as loud as it could. Throngs of scampering creatures quickly crowded around the large fiend, blotting out the moon hanging low in the sky, trampling any residual plant life underfoot. They gazed at each other with heated expressions and dripping fangs. They would join the others near the house in the distance very soon. Apparently they had also sensed something in the house, since they constantly scurried around the building.

The large fiend wondered why they had not

overtaken the prey within already. Even now the earlier arrivals were not trying to break into the house. It watched them merely scuttle back and forth around the perimeter of the building, tapping and scratching with their claws on various sections, moaning to the night sky, growling at each other.

The large fiend swung its baleful gaze back towards the coyote in the distance, still howling to the rising full moon, but decided not to pursue the scrawny animal, despite the deep need to kill any living creature it found. Something in the house promised far more than a morsel of meat.

It growled and grunted and pushed its way to the fore edge of the horde. With unearthly speed and agility the mass of vampires rushed toward the house, over the small hills and dead grass, led by the largest, most ferocious fiend of them all.

17

Brad walked away from Dr. Vinhesier and the little girl. His conscience weighed heavily on his mind, but he still did not stop to look back at them or reconsider, content that he was doing the right thing. He was confident being on his own was the only reason he had managed to stay alive as long as he had.

"Wait," the little girl pleaded.

Despite himself, Brad stopped in his tracks.

"Please, if you must go, then at least take this with you, it could save your life." She reached into her inside pocket and withdrew the same odd-looking device that Brad had used in the library to unlock the mechanism on the book. Its thin arms jutted out from its sides as if ready to clamp down onto the book again.

Brad slowly retraced his steps until he was close enough, reached for the odd key and carefully took it from her.

"What do I need this for?" he asked.

The little girl smiled at him through her tangled hair. "You should hold onto it for now. I would recommend that you retrieve the book as well. Keep them together, keep them apart, but do not allow them to vanish under the moon."

More riddles. Brad certainly did not want to take that terrible book with him, but for some reason he trusted the little girl. He tucked the device into his pocket and slowly began to creep toward the library to get the book. And as he walked away he looked back at the father and daughter he was leaving behind. The love the two of them shared was obvious, and it painfully reminded him of the family that he had lost.

But it also reminded him that even in a world as messed up as this one right now, there were still some things that mattered. There was something even more powerful than vampires or demonic books bent on world domination.

Love.

He turned around again and called out to Dr. Vinheiser and the little girl. "We can make it out of this place if we stick together," he announced. "Come on now, let's get a move on. There's probably not much time left before those things figure out a way in here."

"No," the little girl said somberly. "We cannot go with you. Our place is here, within this house, at this moment in time. Our being together, my father and I, will save us all. We can't expect you to understand, but you must have faith."

Well, it's good to know she understands that I don't understand. But he could not refuse himself the question: "Why on Earth would you want to stay in this place?"

Dr. Vinheiser pushed himself upright as much as he could. "She speaks the truth. We don't expect you to fully understand, in fact I didn't expect her to understand it yet either, but it is now clear to me that she does so, completely."

Brad accepted there was no way he could talk them out of staying behind. Acceptance without understanding had become a familiar feeling to him. It still felt like giving up, each and every time, but he was weary, and could expend no more energy on the incomprehensible pair.

"All right, then," Brad quietly replied. "I respect your wishes, although I do wish you two would leave with me now."

"Good luck," Dr. Vinhesier responded with a

smile. "I have strong faith in your abilities, and know that you will make it."

"Thank you sir," Brad said with an equally bright smile.

Brad turned and walked away again, leaving the little girl and her father behind, oblivious to the absolute absurdity of his sudden change in mood. He was reciting a prayer for them under his breath, hoping to God that they would be all right, but he had to focus on another important matter as well. Getting out of the house alive.

Vampires were collecting in vast numbers around the house, led by the brutally despotic new leader. The others followed its instructions, mainly out of fear. With swift and flawless calculation the vampire leader determined precisely where in the house the humans were located. Every possible escape route from the building was covered completely.

It stood back and watched the others circling the house. Confident in its strategy, it only waited for the right time to strike. The other object he sensed in the house was shielded from its inner vision just enough so it could not completely make out what or where the mysterious prize was.

It was something of great power, and for this reason alone the big brute desired its possession, but it also troubled the fiend to some extent. Why was this object, of all things on this forsaken planet, hidden from perception?

It licked jagged fangs in anticipation, slicing its oily tongue in the process. *So hungry*, as were they all, but patience had gotten them this far, and there was insufficient reason to abandon it now. Until it could determine more about the bigger prize inside the house, and make sure it was not some bait in a clever trap, it would continue to monitor the house and it contained.

Just a little longer.

Brad heard the noises outside the house. The almost gentle scratching of curved talons across the sides of the home was threatening his sanity. But he suspected that was exactly what the vampires were trying to do. If they could cause him to lose control, and possibly jeopardize the lives of the little girl and her father, then they could feed on their minds as well as their bodies.

He was finding it very difficult to locate the library, even though he knew where it was, or had been, or should be. The hallways had grown even longer, stretching far beyond the boundaries of common sense. Walls swayed back and forth as if alive, paintings and pictures distorted into grotesque mockeries of their former grandeur, fixtures flickered on and off, creating a surreal landscape of madness. Brad was too focused on finding his way to wonder where the power was coming from.

A faint greenish smog hung heavily in the air, clogging Brad's nose and stinging his eyes. It was very similar to the stench that the book had emitted in the library. It obstructed his view of what laid before him, yet another of the house's attempt to block his path. *Accepting that now, are you?* he asked himself, but Brad pushed on, motivated by the memory of the little girl and her dying father, and eventually he found the library.

When he pushed the heavy door open at first he did not see the book. The desk sat where it was before, but there was nothing on it, nor on the floor near it. Brad clearly remembered the indentation the book had made when it hit the floor, yet there was no trace of it nearby. Only by searching on his hands and knees did he find the book lying in a far corner of the room underneath several similarly sized volumes. Brad entertained the notion that the book was hiding from him, concealing itself as best it could. He grabbed it, and ignoring the revulsion he felt at the contact, tucked it under his arm and sprinted back out of the room.

The corridors of the house bent and twisted, causing Brad to bang into walls and knock down paintings and pictures. The mist was becoming thicker, disorienting him and draining his energy and will. It invaded every pore in his body, every thought in his mind.

Is it the house? Or perhaps the book? Or maybe they were in conjunction with one another, working in harmony to eliminate the humans who were trying to escape.

Brad found himself stumbling towards the front door. He wanted to turn around and go the other way, but Dr. Vinheiser's words about there not being a rear door anymore resonated in his clouded mind.

But what about the attic? What if he could find a way up into the attic of the house? At least from there he could possibly see outside, perhaps through an air vent or window, and see exactly what the situation outside was, if there were indeed any more vampires roaming about, and if so, how many and where they were.

Despair crept into his planning, and told him even if he could find a way into the attic, which in itself would be difficult and no doubt dangerous, there would be no guarantee that he could even see anything outside. And how would he ever be able to escape the house? Being trapped in a confined space such as an attic was not a wise option.

With great reluctance Brad resigned himself that

his only logical way out of the house was through the front door. He clutched the book to his chest, and hoping it would somehow offer protection of some sort, gripped the splintered chunk of wood he still clutched like a talisman, and slowly walked toward the door.

The scratching noises had diminished to a light scraping here and there. They were still frighteningly deliberate, but were less threatening somehow. Brad thinly hoped that the monsters were disbanding, but reminded himself it was better to be prepared for the worst.

20

Dr. Vinheiser was slipping in and out of consciousness as the little girl cradled his head in her lap, caressing his face and looking into his eyes.

"Father," she whispered. "I am afraid I do not fully understand what my role is going to be. I know only that I am destined to save humanity, and offer myself, my love, for its survival."

Dr. Vinheiser opened his weary eyes and looked at his tiny daughter. He knew very well what must be done, however much it pained his heart and soul. His love was insignificant compared to the importance of the task he must complete.

"I know my child," he moaned softly. "I know. We must be strong, *you* must be strong. Have faith in not only our destinies, but also in our everlasting souls. There is more than this, I am sure of it." He passed out then, eliciting a worried and mournful groan from the little girl.

"Father! Father! Don't leave me. Not now!"

Dr. Vinheiser was roused slightly by her plea, but did not open his eyes. "I am still here child. Fear not. The abominations outside the house must be let in. You must find your way to the front door of the house and release the locks. Hurry now, there is not much time left before the house itself will be directed by the book to destroy us all, and with us, humanity."

The little girl understood. "I love you father," she said through a strained smile.

"And I you, my sweet child. Now go. Hurry along, I say."

Dr. Vinheiser listened as his tiny daughter

scuttled away from him down the hallway. The pain and loneliness that gripped his soul felt cold, but he endured it for the sake of the world. It was the right thing to do. And now all he could do was wait.

The lead vampire bristled with excitement. The change it had detected within the house fueled its hunger. The object was close at hand, very close to where it stood. Soon the prize, and anything else the creature desired, would be for the taking. It reveled in the anticipation that after it had the object in its talons it would be powerful enough to reign over all in this world.

The other vampires jostled back and forth near the front door. Their leader had instructed them to suppress their assaults on the house. They sensed that soon they would gain access to the building and anything inside of it.

22

Brad hesitated at the front door. The three locking mechanisms were within easy reach, yet he did not touch them. Something was holding him back, despite his desperation to escape the house. A cold, impossible breeze from nowhere drifted into his face. Should he unlock the door? Or should he merely play it safe and wait to see if the vampires had completely gone? The book he held was growing heavier with each passing second, and he sensed soon he would no longer be able to carry it.

Brad winced as painful memories crept into his head, rooted to his fear and refusing to relinquish their hold on his mind. It was like being an unwilling audience to a horror film in which he was dashing from one gory scene to the next. Amy was dead. His father was dead. Mrs. Honner was dead. And there was a good chance that everyone he knew was dead.

He fought back the urge to cry, afraid doing so would make him somehow less of a man. An ideal gifted to him by his father. Brad had been able to uphold that ideal his whole life so far, but he knew he was failing now. *There's no point in escaping the house, the old man was right, there's no escape from them.* His head hung heavily and he sobbed.

And then he heard her.

The little girl was running toward him. Her face was a frenzied mixture of relief and sorrow. She knew what she had to do, but was obviously distraught over it.

"Brad!" she cried out to him. "Please, you must not touch the door. You must stay where you are!"

"Don't worry, I'm not going anywhere." The strength had drained from his legs, they felt like rubber, and his head throbbed from hunger and exhaustion. He still held the book, but was ready to drop it. It simply hurt too much to hold on. It felt like it was sliding itself into his mind, latching onto his thoughts, corrupting his humanity.

The house twisted and churned. Walls wavered back and forth, taking on a watery consistency. Everywhere, swirling plumes of fiery gas erupted from the floor, which itself gyrated as if alive. Deep chasms opened up in every room revealing darkness unmatched in its depth and promise of despair.

The little girl was doing her best to make it through the house. She kept her eyes on Brad, and frequently reminded him to stay put and not let go of the book until she reached him.

The floor in front of her opened up into a pitch-black gulf, and the little girl doubled her efforts to reach where Brad sat, helpless. She leapt over the hole, barely landed on the other side and twisted her ankle. She crashed to the floor in pain, but still yelled for Brad to remain where he was.

23

Outside the front door vampires were beginning to mill around with greater urgency. They occasionally fought with each other, but under the watchful eye of their leader, they remained somewhat orderly.

"Remain still!" the leader growled. "The prey are loose within the house, as is the object. We will soon have both."

Another large fiend, nearly as big as the leader, grumbled heavily, its foul breath causing even the other vampires to shrink back in disgust.

"We should attack immediately," it snarled, blood-red eyes glaring with hatred. "We are wasting time strolling around here like foolish cattle. There is food inside, only separated from us by flimsy walls and glass. We must act now!"

"Silence!" the leader commanded. "The object within is far more important than another paltry meal."

The other vampires, fearing the wrath of their leader, glared at the outspoken one. By the sheer weight of their numbers they silenced it forever, nourishing themselves on its deformed body and twisted mind.

24

Dr. Vinheiser's eyes rolled back in his head; he was having trouble staying awake. His injuries were fatal, but he had to stay alert as long as he could. He had to make sure that his daughter made it to the front door of the house. He had to make sure she would let the vampires in.

The little girl crawled across the shifting floors, slowly making her way to Brad, who sat on the treacherous floor, the book clutched fast to his body, his head hanging over it in despair. Time was running out. Soon the vampires would release their pent up rage and power and assault the house right down to its very foundation, utterly destroying all those within and humanity's last chance at survival.

Brad's mind was losing the battle with the book. The *Tome* was conquering his will, inducing his mind to disbelieve any of this was happening.

"It's all right," he happily chanted over and over again. "No real problems here, just make-believe ones. We'll be just fine. Just fine."

The little girl crawled as fast as she could across the buckling floor. The house hindered her at every opportunity, slid furniture toward her, dropped drywall down on her from above. "Hang on Brad," she cried. "I'm almost there."

Brad just hummed to himself as if he were all alone. His mind was only occupied with pleasant thoughts. Memories of his father in happier times, of Amy strolling down the sidewalk, her hair flowing around her pretty face. What the world had been like before.

The vampire leader finally abandoned patience when it sensed the object in the house was very near to the front door. The book was calling out to it, sending out a beacon that it was on the other side of the door. Compelled to action, he ordered the others to attack.

They began to thrash violently against the front door. It was made of wrought iron, nearly four inches thick, but they did not care. They, too, sensed the presence of a strange and powerful object within the house, and their lust for blood and power would not be denied. With great, unyielding blows they relentlessly assaulted the last barrier in their way.

The little girl heard the vampires outside the door, and she re-doubled her efforts to reach Brad before it was too late.

"I'm coming. I'm coming," she cried. "Please don't move. And whatever you do, don't open the door!"

Brad barely heard her. He was becoming lost within the lies of the book.

His mind swayed back and forth, between reality and insanity, between the false utopia the book offered and the real danger he was in. He no longer knew the difference, or cared for that matter. More and more his only concern was holding onto the book, making sure it was safe from harm, doing what it told him to do. He cradled it in his arms, caressing it lovingly. He hardly felt the thin, curved talon slice into the back of his neck. One of the vampires had breached the front door, and managed to slip one of its claws through the opening.

Warm, rich blood dripped down Brad's back, soaking his tattered shirt and pooling on the floor. The vampires smelled the blood and increased their assault on the door. Heavy crashes echoed throughout the house as the fiends relentlessly tried to get at their prey. Slate-gray hands tipped with two-inch, dirt-encrusted claws reached around every corner of the door, swatting at the air in vain attempts to grab anything within reach.

Just as the leader's huge claw ripped clean through the door and reached for Brad's throat, the little girl fell across his lap and tore the book from his hands.

25

"It's all right now," the little girl whispered into Brad's ear. "Everything will be all right now."

Brad's vision was blurred and he had trouble making out exactly who, or what, was standing above him. His back ached and his legs were so cramped he could hardly move, but his memory, his mind, was gradually coming back to him, and with them his free will.

"W…what's going on?" he mumbled. "Where am I?"

The little girl smiled down at him and helped him to his feet. "We're still in my father's house, near the front door."

Brad stood up, brushed himself off, felt the bloody wound on his neck. The pain was dull, but still enough to warrant his attention. He ripped off a piece of his shirt and wrapped it around the wound.

"What happened to those things that were trying to get inside? Where are they?"

The polluted breath on the back of his neck stung his wound and drove fear straight into his soul. Too afraid to turn around he merely stood where he was and waited for the inevitable response to his questions.

"Yes, foolish one," the raspy voice slurred. "We are here."

They speak English? Brad stared at the little girl. She was still standing in front of him, oddly she was still smiling. The thought that somehow she, too, could be connected with the vampires occurred to Brad, but he pushed it aside. Her own father lay in another part of the house dying. Surely the little girl had not forgotten about him.

Brad decided if he was going to die, then he at

least wanted to understand why.

"What is going on here?" he demanded to know. "Are you a part of this?" he asked the little girl.

The little girl merely looked deep into his eyes and tilted her head. She did not speak, nor make any attempt to escape. And something inside of Brad told him that she had as little to do with the invasion as he did.

The vampires were collecting inside of the house, filling the rooms with their grotesque bodies and evil intentions. The leader moved forward and wrapped its long arms around Brad in an iron grip. Brad could not move a muscle or even cry out in pain. He was as helpless as a newborn baby. Just when he was about to pass out, the fiend suddenly dropped him to the floor.

"Little one," it drawled. "Before my minions and I take pleasure in your pain and death you shall willingly hand over the object you are so obviously hiding behind your puny back." The creature's long sinewy arms flailed high above its deformed head, smacked into the ceiling.

Why doesn't it just take the book from her? Brad wondered.

"Give me the object now!" the leader commanded with even more authority than before. "Do as I say!"

Brad could see the thing clenching its fists in rage. Finally, it calmed and crossed its arms, observing the little girl as it did so.

"I see. We'll just have to feed first. There will be time after the feast for the other."

Swiftly it gestured for the multiplying vampires who were filing into the house to line up in an organized fashion. They obeyed without question, only mumbling animalistic grunts.

Brad watched helplessly as the monsters scooped up the little girl and threw her into the far corner of the room. She smacked hard into the wall, but still managed to hold onto the book.

She looked up at Brad, her battered face covered in blood. "Everything will be all right," she repeated to him. "Everything will be all right."

Slowly, the vampires advanced, savouring their victory. Brad managed to stand up only to be knocked back across the room by a particularly short, stocky vampire. It gloated screeched with joy at its successful assault.

When Brad came to, he felt cold breath that smelled like an open grave on his face. There were at least a dozen hideous expressions inches away from him, studying him, sizing him up.

"Well, what are you waiting for, an invitation?" he screamed defiantly. His father had taught him never to go down without a fight, and he was going to honor that advice. He laughed to himself when the grainy image of his drunken father materialized above the hideous expressions leering at him. He imagined his father started scolding him for not looking after his little sister.

"It wasn't my fault dad," he moaned. "Those things took her before I knew what happened." And then the image faded as suddenly as it had come, leaving only the pale faces of the creatures staring at him with hunger in their eyes and black drool dripping from their gaping mouths.

The vampire leader casually strolled over to where the little girl lay on the floor. He bent down next to her as a loving parent would its child, an evil grin plastered across his pale face.

"And now, my dear," he whispered with a wink. "Give me the object. If you do as I say, you may yet die quickly. Otherwise your passing will be most unpleasant, as will your friend's."

The little girl said nothing. She merely looked up into the vampire's snarling face and stared into the soulless, empty eyes. The depth within those eyes was bottomless, like the cold abyss the vampires came from.

"Very well young foolish one," the leader grumbled in disgust. "You have sealed your own fate then. We will have the object soon enough."

The little girl turned her head to one side as if she were actually offering her throat to the fiend. Brad watched, horrified as the huge vampire grinned an impossibly wide smile, from pointed ear to pointed ear, and gripped the little girl's neck in his elongated fingers. Without a sound, and with all of the other vampires looking on, the leader sank his massive, yellowed fangs into her throat.

26

Brad looked past the grotesque faces towering above him to the little girl who was lying on her back with nearly a dozen of the creatures standing above her. The leader apparently had taken his fill, and he slowly stood and sauntered towards the front door. He bumped into a nearby wall and fell to the floor, struggled to stand back up.

Brad wondered if the leader was ill, or better yet, if he were dying. But there were still dozens of other vampires. Too weak to fight, he could only hope that his own death would be quick and painless, although he knew that it probably would not be.

All of the vampires started howling at the top of their lungs. The very walls and ceiling shook from the sheer volume of their cries, dust cascaded down over everything inside the house.

Brad watched as the vampires, which a moment before had appeared to be his impending executioners, fell to the ground. They writhed and twisted in pain unlike anything he had ever seen before. Despite his long-standing hatred for them, he felt a pang of empathy. But only a little one. As soon as he could, he got to his feet and stumbled over to where the little girl lay. She did not move.

"Are you all right?" he asked as he fell to his knees. "Please tell me you're all right. Please. You have to be."

The little girl opened her eyes and looked up at Brad. Her face was puffed where bruises were already coloring, and her one arm was twisted behind her back in an unnatural way. Brad knew it was definitely broken.

"Do not worry about me," she moaned. "You must take the book out of the house and bury it in consecrated ground. You must smear the pages with holy water. You must believe in its destruction fully, with every fiber in your body and every part of your soul. You must." She pulled the book out from behind her back, and held it out to Brad.

Brad wrenched the book from her hands, and was surprised by just how strong her grip was. It was like trying to take something forcibly from a grown man.

"Was your father really responsible for all this?" he asked. He had to know. He would never be able to rest if he did not know what had caused the terrible holocaust.

"Yes, my father was responsible," the little girl said quietly.

"What's happening to the vampires now?"

"Their race dwelled for eons, knowing that they would have a chance on Earth eventually. All vampires need blood to survive, and each one is linked to another." The little girl paused momentarily, wiped her eyes and then continued.

"After my father realized what he had done, what the book had used him to do, he set out to remedy the problem. He did manage to complete his work, but did not have time to apply it. The book made it difficult for him to concentrate."

Brad understood about that, now. "But what work did he complete? And what is killing the vampires?" Almost before he finished the sentence, it occurred to him.

It was her blood! The vampire started to die after he drank it.

Brad struggled to speak. "You... were the solution," he whispered. "They started dying after the big one drank your blood."

"My father would have been pleased to know it worked. Humanity is safe."

"Your father," Brad suddenly cried. "We have to go back for him. He could still be alive."

The little girl smiled as best she could. "No, he has passed on. I can feel it. And the house, the book, would make it rather difficult to reach him now."

Brad nodded. The house was still twisting and bending, and the chances of reaching Dr. Vinheiser again were slim. The chasm she had leapt minutes before now nearly split the area they were in from the rest of the house. He stood up and stepped over the remains of the vampires. Most had already been reduced to filthy piles of fine ash, black and acrid, and the ones still alive only faintly resembled the fiendish monsters they had been.

"But how did all of the vampires die if only the leader actually drank your blood?"

"They are all linked to one another," the little girl sighed. "They are all linked..." Her eyes rolled back in her head.

Brad tried to rouse her, then just held her tightly in his arms.

No, no! The pain he felt was only rivaled by the time he lost his little sister. In a way, he had begun to think of the little girl in the same way. Like Amy, she was innocent and frail, too young to survive the horrible affliction that the world faced.

27

Brad struggled to carry her and the book out the front door, but he could not chance leaving either of them behind in the house. He walked between the patches of ichor and ash for a long while before he set her down on the ground, far away from the house. He pulled off what was left of his shirt and wadded it up under her head. She clearly did not need a pillow now, but he thought she would have appreciated the gesture anyway.

Tears of grief and relief streamed down his face as Brad realized he had not asked Dr. Vinheiser the one question he should have. "You willingly sacrificed your life to destroy the vampires, to save us all, and I don't even know your name," Brad sobbed apologetically.

Long after his dehydrated body ran dry of tears, Brad ran out of energy to cry any more, and he stood and looked around what once had been beautiful fields and woods. The dead landscape was littered with the countless remains of the vampires, as far as the eye could see in all directions. Corrupt black dust spilled out of their rotted clothes, grotesque epitaphs to their brief and savage reign.

Brad shuddered as he contemplated the number of fiends that had been waiting outside the house. He realized had Dr. Vinheiser not completed his work, not sacrificed his daughter, there would have been no escape from the house, from the vampires, from any of it.

A gentle but steady wind began to pick up from the east, carrying with it the remains of the vampires far into the horizon. Brad watched the vague, blackish taint in the air as the ashes mingled with the wind. It swirled with the breeze, and could have been beautiful were it not for its nature.

Brad wondered how many people had survived. Surely there must be some others somewhere. He would have to find them, help them, anyway he could. Tell them about *her*, Dr. Vinheiser's solution.

But his first duty was to destroy the book, the curse that unleashed this nightmare in the first place. The little girl had told him how to do it, and he was going to make sure he did, just the way she said. He owed it to her, the old man, himself, the world, to destroy the key to the door between our world and... Brad's blood froze as he realized there could be more fiends, more evil which the book could unleash upon the Earth.

He thought hard and recalled an old church he had passed by before. It had to be about a dozen miles away, but he would find a way to make it there. He remembered how empty it seemed, with nothing but darkness seeping out its foggy, cracked windows. He reluctantly lifted the giant tome, which seemed to be slippery, hard to grip, as the pale promise of sunrise brightened the sky, but did not yet color it.

A shudder ran up his spine when he also recalled how there were some strange noises coming from behind the building, inhuman noises, which sounded like something was being torn apart.

He could only hope that all of the vampires, everywhere, were truly linked with those here.

…The Colour of Time

by K.R. Gentile

Buried

Marcus pulled the last of the IV bags from his "emergency" kit, hanging it from the low ceiling of the tiny crawlway on one of the hooks mounted there for just this occurrence. The small light of the battery lamp was growing dimmer as the last needle pierced his flesh and he unblocked the drip feed. Seventeen various bags hung around him, feeding chems through their needles into his flesh, with settings ranging from steady streams to single drops per week.

It had been hours since the last sounds came from above, since the last rubble had settled. But Marcus had seen all this before it had happened; he had been ready for it. He removed his clothing and sat in lotus on the bare stone floor, cold to the touch, but that was necessary as well, and there would be no discomfort in a while. He began deep breaths, cycling his chakra in the desired pattern, an alignment taught only to the most advanced students of Yoga. As he began to breathe deeper, he watched the sands of the small hourglass positioned so he could see it. As he watched the sand flowed as a stream… then a broken trickle… then as individual grains…

Then the sand stopped…

Birth

Donald Jamison paced back and forth, tethered to the desk by the short, black phone cord. "Look… I don't give a damn what the president said. The appropriation numbers *are* correct, and he'll make sure congress forks it over, or he can deal with the damn Russkies without my help… there's no reason why I can't sell to them instead!"

A short knock at the door caught his attention and the white-clad nurse came into the room. "Mister Jamison… you should come now, your wife is asking for you. There have been… complications."

"Well you tell him I'll call him back when I'm damn good and ready!" the head of Jamison Dynamics shouted as he slammed the phone back into the cradle. "Complications," he muttered as the nurse led him toward the master wing of the house. "That woman's been a complication since Dad pushed her into my bed." The nurse sighed but said nothing else as they walked down the carpeted halls of the mansion. After all, she needed the job.

The Jamison family doctor met them at the door. "Mister Jamison, we should talk before you step in."

Donald Jamison locked the doctor with a withering stare. "Don't you presume to tell me what to do in MY house, you quack," and with that said, he opened the door and stalked into the room. "What the hell is it, Miriam? You know I was on the phone with the Pres-" his voice paused as one of the nurses carefully draped the sheet over Miriam Jamison's face. The bedclothes were soaked a deep red about her hips and legs. The Doctor stepped into Jamison's view.

"We did everything we could, but the birth was difficult. Perhaps if we had been allowed to move her to the hospital-"

"Seven generations of Jamisons have been born in *this* house, in *that* bed... I'm not about to break that tradition."

The doctor looked as though he had been slapped, and one of the nurses left the room at a run. "Good God, Donald, your wife is has just died giving birth, and you're talking about family tradition?"

"Doctor, if I want moralist viewpoints, I'll buy a priest's opinion. If the woman had been strong enough, she'd still be here. Now, show me my sons."

The Doctor shook his head. "Son, actually. The other was delivered with the umbilical around his neck, which was broken. These things... err... can happen without the *proper* medical facilities."

Donald stepped past him. "And a good deal more money as well, I suppose." One of the nurses stepped forward with a baby swaddled in blankets and offered the child to Donald, who made no move to take his son into his arms. "Why is the boy not crying? All babies cry when born, don't they?" He looked at the child, catching a glimpse of blue eyes from under the child's eyelids for a moment.

"It's common, sir, but not always the case. The child cleared his lungs and then quieted immediately. That's the sign of a strong child."

"As he damn well should be... he's a Jamison,

after all. Thank God he took after me and not that… weakling." Jamison turned to one of the servants. "Take the child to his nursery and have the nanny begin attending to him immediately." He began to leave, when the doctor grabbed his arm.

"Sir, about your wife and other son?"

Donald snorted. "Leave them; the staff will make arrangements to have them buried in the family plots. I suppose it's the least I should do since she managed to give me *one* good child in exchange for all the money she spent."

Donald Jamison returned to his office, sat down and took several peppermint swirl candies from the goblet on his desk, popping them into his mouth.

The door opened, and Robert Smythton entered quietly. The family lawyer opened his briefcase and withdrew several papers. "Donald, a few small matters before you get back to work."

Donald Jamison sighed, letting the taste of the mint sooth his nerves. "What now?"

The lawyer set a form down. "First, this authorizes the payment of the nursing and delivery staff."

Donald looked over it and signed it. "Call the medical board as well. If that quack is still practicing in Massachusetts by the end of the week, I'll have all of them dismissed." Smythton nodded, accustomed to the extreme demands of his richest client after years of ministering to his legal needs.

"And lastly, the birth certificate. Miriam, bless her soul, did not have time to name the child."

"Marcus. He'll be named after my great-grandfather." He gestured toward the painting of the stern looking military officer dominating one wall. "It's a good family name, traces back to Rome. He fought as a mercenary in India with the British, during the quelling of the Revolt, you know." He gazed at the peppermint swirl in his palm and then popped it into his mouth, picking up the phone.

Fast Forward…

Beach

Peppermint made a last adjustment to the silenced THP .22 semi-auto in his ankle holster and smoothed down the velvet crimson trouser leg, taking one last glance at the pant leg's lay. Its twin already lay sheathed on his other leg. A quick adjustment of the Italian cuffs on his black silk shirt and a brush of the lapels of his trademark jacket and he stepped out on to the deserted strip of beach along the edge of Devil's Cape and toward the waiting figure of Hans Drumhellsen, impeccably dressed, if slightly ominous, in his black suit and high-tech face plate.

The white tie's a nice touch.

Peppermint nodded in agreement as he approached.

The strip was deserted in the twilight, and plenty of open beach stretched in either direction. More than enough to give someone a sense of security… right before the killing blow struck. But he liked Hans for some reason, and he knew She was there was well. The practiced smile crept onto his face.

Careful, my love… do not underestimate him… his words can kill. I would suggest a single shot through each eye lens, that should disable him and the device he uses for fine control of his ability, then a third through his voice box to take it away permanently, the voice of his mistress sang to him. He smiled a silent thanks for Her advice, reminding her he had been doing this for a while now, but that he was grateful for it all the same.

"So, Hans... I was just wondering if one of us is going swimming?"

Rewind…

Dog

Marcus followed the faint whining to a small patch of grass and broken concrete in a small clearing behind the shrubs. There he found a small dirty pile of brown fur with dim eyes and a graying muzzle. The old dog, one of the numerous strays that circled the walls of Boston's Naceworth Estates, was a small shivering barely moving lump of bones. A bowl of old food lay less than five feet from its nose. As Marcus approached, he could see that all four of the dog's legs had been broken. As he knelt he could tell the dog had been here for days, taunted by the food and water just out of reach. Tears began to well in Marcus' eyes, as he heard Her voice.

You know what to do, my love, She said to him. *The animal will never survive the long trip to the healer. Release the poor creature - just as I showed you - so that it may live again.*

Marcus placed his small hand on the dog's nose, and received a plaintive dry brush of tongue and a weak wag of a tail at his touch. He moved the water bowl and held the dog's head up gingerly, as it took a few laps at the water… confirming the dog was simply too tired to even quench its thirst. Gently, he petted the dog's head and neck, tears running down his face at the plight of the abused animal. "Is this a Good Death?" Marcus asked.

The motherly voice replied. *The best, child… the best.*

With a quick motion Marcus snapped the dog's neck, and as merciful as the movement it was, it seemed both perverse and abhorrent, being performed with such skill by the hands of a nine-year old child.

Fast Forward…

College

"So, why do you take it, Marc?" Samantha asked as she propped herself up on a pillow, sweat beaded on her brow. "All the crap Hawthorne and his little pack of dogs give you?"

Marcus smiled. "Because I'm better than them, luv. I'm nineteen years old, speak seven languages and just completed my Master's in Abnormal Psychology." He chuckled and lit two cigarettes, handing one off to the statuesque blond 16 years his elder. "And regardless of what petty little things they say about me, I can smile it all away because in the end *they* need *me*, not the other way around." He licked his lips and closed his eyes, allowing the euphoria to begin washing over him. Samantha inhaled sharply as the first wave of the drugs hit her as well.

"He keeps calling me, you know, asking me out, things like tha… WOW…these are *fantastic*."

"Simple enough to make. Blend the marijuana with some pipe tobacco to neutralize the hemp's odor, and it passes most police inspections. And the euphoric is in the solution soaked into the filter, and not the cigarette itself, so even if they test the filling, nothing but a little extra 'kick' and well below even the most stringent legal limit."

She chuckled, "And since you developed the… what did you call it?"

"Smooth Jazz."

"Yes… the Jazz. Since you developed it yourself, it's not illegal because it doesn't even exist.

A perfectly legal high… but it would still get me fired."
Samantha looked serious for a moment. "You do
realize that, Marc? This is fun, and I really enjoy it.
But if my husband, my -- well if anyone -- ever found
out, my life would be over. Just the scandal alone of
a tenured professor sleeping with a student would be
enough-"

Marcus touched his finger to her lips. "It'll never
happen, luv."

Samantha pulled the finger away. "I'm serious,
Marcus. This has to end, eventually, no reprisals, no
occasional rekindling. Promise me that when it
comes to a close, you'll end it clean."

Marcus smiled and took another draw from the
cigarette. "I promise. When it's over, I'll end it clean."
He stubbed the remnant out in the ashtray.

"Now, let me tell you about this new project. I call
it 'Vishnu'…"

Rewind...

Tommy

Tommy Bellingham screamed in his annoyingly shrill voice as Marcus knelt on the kicking child's leg. Tommy had always been a turd-head at school, and Marcus had always thought his voice was like a little girl's. Several quick smashes with the ball-peen hammer and Tommy's left knee finally shattered under the blows. Marcus sat back as Tommy whimpered, flailing at the destroyed knee with limbs flapping like rubber straps, each joint no longer capable of supporting the child's weight. Marcus stood and brushed off his Sunday pants, making sure no dust from the garage floor would be left to make Mommy Kate angry.

Tommy stopped whining and yelled again. "You freak! When I tell my dad he'll make you pay, Marcus Jamison. He'll... he'll... he'll... S - U - E... *SUE* you and take all the money your Dad stole from the government!"

Marcus opened his backpack and took out the brown bag from the grocery story, setting the pencils and notebook aside. Stepping next to Tommy's head he carefully paced out five feet and set the dog bowl down. In it he placed the fresh hamburger and French-fries, and then looked to Tommy. "You like ketchup a lot, don't you?" he asked in friendly tone.

"Go to hell, Marcus! You go to hell and eat the devil's hotdog like you your real momma's doing!"

Marcus stopped and looked at Tommy for a second, then put the ketchup bottle down next to the bowl. "There's no devil, Tommy. My mommy's someone else's little girl now, any stupid-head knows that." He stepped back and pulled the chair over to where he could see both the crippled child and the bowl of food, and sat down. "Everything's right?" he asked aloud.

His teacher's voice replied from the shadows. *Perfect, my child, you've done everything exactly right. You always do, because you're such a good student.*

Marcus beamed at the praise, and then opened the fresh composition book writing "day one" and tomorrow's date at the top of the page. Then he closed the book and set it carefully on the chair, collecting his things. "I'll see you tomorrow, Tommy. If you get hungry, it's right there. No pickles, just like you always get." The heavy garage door cut off the child's pleading, and Marcus carefully locked the door and put the key back under the rock, where the Hendersons always kept it when they vacationed for the summer. As he knelt, a puppy wandered up and Marcus patted his head. The puppy's tail wagged, and Marcus wondered if he saw some recognition in the dog's eyes. "What do we call this exercise, Ma'am?"

Why Marcus, did I forget to tell you? The smiling voice replied. *This is called Justice, my love. Now run on home before your parents worry.*

Rewind…

Womb

Warmth, floating, love, food, *another*?
Touch, feel, caress, *Another.*
Mirror images, soft fingers, bumping, red, warm *Another*!
Heat, anger, hate, fingers reach, touch, feel, grasp, pull, pull harder, PULL HARDER, TWIST, JERK, PULL HARDER!
Silence.
Alone.

Clean End

Marcus smoothed the blond hair back away from the woman's face, as the last vestiges of her ravaged neurons fired, the overdose shutting down her autonomic functions. The needle still dangled from her shackled arms. He carefully positioned the newspaper on the floor near the empty bottle of illegal barbiturates, displaying the headline "Harvard Medical Professor implicated in sex/drug scandal…" and scattered a few loose pills around it. Davis Hawthorn's body still sat in the chair, his face wiped clean by the "self-inflicted" shotgun blast, the room still smelled slightly of cordite. After one last glance, he zippered the bondage mask closed over Samantha's contorted face.

"As I promised, it ends clean between us, luv."

Foundation

"With this first shovel of dirt, we break ground on the new site of the Church of the Purified Mind. All views are welcome!" The crowd applauded as Doctor Marcus Jamison raised the shovel in a triumphant gesture and then handed it to his aid, Doctor Indera Kalammni.

As the mayor of Pinnacle City approached the podium, Marcus took his seat and Indera leaned over to him, her silky black hair smelling lightly of jasmine, her white suit in sharp contrast with her cinnamon colored skin. "Fifth row, with the simply *horrid* red tie."

Marcus smiled and looked out, surveying the crowd. "Ah…" he said as he spotted the uncomfortable looking man with the barely concealed camera. The man stood out like a sore thumb in the sea of fab fashion statements of the posh crowd of 1970's movers, shakers and stars. "… I see him."

Indera smiled brightly, "One of Mand's hounds, Darling?"

Marcus chuckled. "Hardly, luv. Werner would have castrated him for standing out this badly. My guess is FBI… possibly Treasury."

They smiled and Marcus waved, acknowledging some unremarkable joke the mayor had made.

"Should I have Heinrich speak to the gentleman privately?" she nodded to the large Aryan fellow standing toward the back of the gathering. Heinrich was ex East-German KGB, and one of Indera's stable of loyal security operatives for the newly founded Church.

"I don't think that's necessary, luv. Just find out who he is and whose hand is on the leash. After all, we wouldn't want any surprises in Prague later this week, now would we?" Marcus stood again, and retook the podium to close the proceedings and open the bar.

Fast Forward…

Collections

"Now, Director Mand, you know that you're not supposed to have coffee after six p.m.," the secretary at the desk scolded as she took the pot from him. "How about some nice Earl Grey?" Werner Mand looked her right in the eye and smiled broadly, like someone's kindly grandfather at Christmas time.

"How about you shove that tea up your ass and give me the fucking coffee before I put a .45 ACP sphincter in the center of your forehead?"

The secretary almost snapped back when she saw something in the old man's eyes that reminded her a bit too much of a cobra she saw in the Pinnacle City Zoo's reptile house. She closed her mouth and quickly relinquished the carafe.

Pleased with himself, Werner took the whole pot with him to make a statement. As he made for his office with his trophy he nodded in salute to the Guards at his office door, one a Marine the other a Thunderbolt Operator, both dressed in civvies but their demeanor broadcasting their true selves from a mile away. He winked to them. "I'll give you both a hundred bucks if you strangle her, dress her like a hooker and throw her in a dumpster outside the mayor's office… after all, not like it'd be the first time they found one there." Both chuckled a bit as he closed the door.

As he sat town, he winced at the pain in his back. Twenty-two years as a CIA field operative and another quarter century in various positions as he climbed the ladder to Director of Joint Operations Command could do that to a man. At sixty-seven, time was finally catching up with him. He sorted through some papers and signed off on an operation between Basilisk and Thunderbolt in the Blackguard Isles. "Red Web Syndicate. Bloody 'spiders' again… we should nuke the entire island chain and start over."

"I'm surprised you haven't, Werner."

Werner spun toward the voice, the .45 SOCOM Mk23 clearing the secret holster under the desk in a blur that would surprise most of the yacht club. But leveled, the weight of the heavy automatic was wrong. Ejecting the clip and flipping it over, Werner saw it was empty. One by one the rounds bounced out onto the desk from the shadows. He set the empty pistol down on the desk next to the stack of bullets.

"You got a name? I like to know the name of the man I'm about to sign up for decades of enforced jailhouse sodomy."

A ghost walked out of the shadows.

"Peppermint?"

"In the flesh, luv," Marcus chuckled. The new SIN-designed fighting suit was even better at dispersing shadows than his old body suit, if less comfortable than his preferred turtleneck and chinos. "You look good, Werner. And Director? My, my, who did you kill and/or sleep with for this cushy desk job?"

Werner eased back in his seat. "I'd ask how, but I stopped asking crap like that after I got a glance at Thunderbolt's 'Project: PARAGON' Budget."

"Do you remember the message I sent you in Barni, Werner?" Peppermint circled the desk and sat on the corner.

Werner sighed. "So, here to collect on the bill?" He saw Peppermint nod. "It's about time." Then everything went black.

Rewind...

Vietnam

"Are you out of your fucking mind, Jamison?" Werner Mand slammed the file down on the desk. "Good God… torture, murder, even rape I can deal with. Hell, I'll even charter Air America to fly in the fucking beer and coke and we'll make a party out of it… but medical experimentation on American soldiers? There's a line, idiot and you just crossed it. How the fuck am I gonna square this with MAC-V-SOG?"

"Werner, have a seat. Want a drink or something, luv? You have to watch your fluid levels in the jungle, you know." Marcus offered a glass of water, only for it to be slapped out of his hand to crash against the wall. A raised hand stopped the three Montagnards, their bush-swords already drawn and in fighting positions.

"Nice, Marcus… let me guess, you've got the natives believing that existential crap you blather on about. Christ… first Kurtz, now you? What the fuck are you guys smoking in this jungle?"

"Werner, when you're done, wake me okay?" Mand gave him the finger and Marcus chuckled. "Look, you said get the operation done however I could right? Well, that's what I'm doing."

Mand cut a disgusted look at the folder on the table. "I've read the fucking file, you lunatic. Explain to me how drug-amplified Green Berets running mercenary operations for the Triads in Hong Kong is going to stop the fucking war in Vietnam?"

"Because, luv, if we provide security for the drug

shipments from Afghanistan and Columbia, they won't need the security from the Cong and the NA. Without that need, their support money dries up and this puts pressure on the Chinese and the Russians to stop sending 'advisors' here and forces them to put those elsewhere. And with no weapons and support, you can own Vietnam in a matter of months. See? Everyone happy."

"Except then we'll be personally responsible for the UNITED STATES FUCKING ARMY RUNNING DRUGS FOR THE CHINESE FUCKING MAFIA!" Mand screamed.

Marcus winced. "A little louder, Werner, please. I don't think they heard you in Da Nang."

Werner started to say something but Marcus stopped him.

"Look, luv. That's the beauty of my operation, Werner. Once the war is over, we simply 'activate' the enforcers we've sent, and they kill everyone involved and then themselves."

Werner's mind shut down for a second. "They what?"

"Come now, Werner, did you think I wouldn't cover our flag enshrouded asses?" Marcus glided around the desk and sat down on the edge and smiled.

"Werner, all the 'HK Cowboys' – that's what I'm calling them – they have a special mental conditioning. One code word from us and they activate, carrying out a carefully prepared subset of actions due to embedded mental conditioning. They'll begin to take out their contacts as targets, move on up the food chain and destroy the entire super-structure of the Triads, as well as any connections they made along way. And then, when each operative has gotten as far as they can, they frag themselves. It's a self-contained solution, nice and neat."

"Marcus, I want you to shut this down now."

"I'm sorry, what?"

"You heard me, Marcus," Werner said, punctuating his order by drawing his pistol and quickly shooting the three native bodyguards before Marcus could give any signal to them. "Lock it down, lock everything down. We burn this place to the ground and you take some fucking time and vanish."

"But, Werner-"

Mand leveled the Colt at Marcus's head.

"Shut. It. Down."

Zig-Zag

"Vitals are stable, pupils unresponsive, no pain response, one-hundred percent vegetative state." Dr. Bryans checked off a few things and then signed on the form on the clipboard. Officer Taggart checked the restraints, and Bryans looked over. "Are those really necessary, Dave? This *is* the most secure level five prison in the US."

Taggart shrugged, "Doesn't matter, Doc. Patrioteer says they stay handcuffed, they stay handcuffed."

"If you ask me, I think his helmet's gotten a little tight," Bryans chuckled. "Anyway, time to leave sleeping beauty here for another day. Four more stops and I'll buy you coffee." Bryans opened the door and stared down the muzzle of a high-tech auto-pistol. It was the last thing he saw as the Hobo Spider operative pulled the trigger.

Taggart kicked the door of the med-cell closed, the lock engaging home automatically as he slammed his hand on the big red panic button.

Outside he heard sporadic gunfire, and the gruff order to "cut it open" as a jet of flames burst from above the lock where a cutting torch was being used. He drew his service pistol and put it next to the comatose man's head. "Well buddy, it's obviously you they're after. Sorry 'bout this." He pulled the trigger.

Nothing happened.

Pulling the pistol back, he jacked the slide and pulled the trigger again.

Again, nothing happened.

The gun was fine, but his finger simply would not pull the trigger. He felt the wetness on his face. A smear of blood coated his fingers as he pulled them away from his face, a stream trickling from his nostril. His gaze returned to the bed, the coma patient was looking at him.

"W-water."

Taggart felt confused and poured a cup of water and handed it to the awakening patient. Then he looked at him again, and Taggart found himself helping the man lift himself from the bed, becoming a statue as the man got to his feet. He watched, frozen, as the man executed several stretches, each more complicated than the previous, bones and joints cracking as they limbered out after years of immobility. Finally, he stood on his own and looked into Taggart's eyes.

"Thanks for the support," the patient said as he cocked his hand back, his fingers held flat like blade or spear point.

Officer Taggart swore he saw it glow before it punched through his skull.

As the lock clattered to the floor, Marcus turned around and smiled at the shocked Red Web Syndicate gunmen.

"What kept you, luv?"

Incense

"What do you mean, what kept me?" Incense growled through clinched teeth dropping over the short wall, followed all-to-closely by a spray of bullets and a sharp burst of Spanish cursing.

Dr. Peppermint chuckled at her, taking a moment to kiss her deeply. She reloaded her twin Czech Skopions. "All I meant is that Julio seems to have gone to a bit of trouble arranging this party for us, and I've been here for ten minutes already." He chuckled as he eased his way around the edge, taking a peek. He snapped back as bullets tore into the masonry of the low stucco wall. "Hmmm… do you think you can chat them up a bit for me, luv? I'm running out of small talk."

In a quick, practiced, movement Incense jacked the slides on both machine pistols, one after the other. "Sure, they seem like nice gents," she said in her sweet voice, the mixed English and Farsi accents dripping like caramel from a cinnamon roll. She popped up, sweeping the twin pistols in twin infinity symbols across the courtyard, and in the light of the tracers she could see Peppermint, already over the wall and into the midst of the startled gunmen, a deadly black shadow in his fighting suit, only his red hair and face barely visible in the twilight.

Until he reached the gunmen.

With a deep breath, Peppermint dropped to the ground and rolled to his feet fixing the group with his glare. Something happened as he whispered dark terrible things to them, and the men stopped stock still. He was moving in between them. It was as if time stopped for them, as their minds tried to digest what he told them, their darkest thought laid open to them, bare and raw. As his blows landed, Incense could see the glow around his hands. Where each of those deadly talented hands touched, there was a ripple in the air and the sounds of snapping bones and shattering spines. Within moments half the courtyard was full of the broken dolls of Columbian gunmen, and the rest were just beginning to register the violence being perpetrated upon them. Incense flipped her selectors to semi-auto and carefully began to snap-shoot at the men still standing as Peppermint danced between them, his art a flowing combination of Krav Maga, jujutsu, and Hindi Kalarippayattu, all enhanced by his own innate talents. The fight was over as quickly as it had begun, and the gunmen lay dead or dying throughout the courtyard.

Without looking, Peppermint addressed the overlooking balcony. "Well, Julio? Do you feel this is sufficient for the audition?"

The swarthy drug lord stepped out, clapping slowly, flanked by armed guards on either side. "Very nice, my friend… but this 'Church' of yours. How do the students compare to the teacher?"

Incense laughed as Julio's bodyguards on either side dropped to the ground, the balcony suddenly filled with hooded figures, each holding a *Rumal*, the ritual strangler's weapon of the Thuggie Cult, the variously colored length of each having silently incapacitated one of Julio's bodyguards as they stood next to him.

"Any other questions, my dear Julio?"

Rewind...

Peppermints

Marcus sat on the other side of the desk, feeling disgusted as his stepmother Kate plopped into his father's chair. "The answer is no, Marcus. No more money... maybe your father felt like he needed to support college surfing but no more. Get out there and start a practice, like anyone normal."

He sighed. "I have a job, Kate, and to be honest with you, it's *my* money, not yours."

Kate's face contorted as she dug her long fingernails into the goblet of peppermint candies, popping several into her mouth. "Don't you dare call me by my first name, Marcus. I'm your mother and I won't be talked to-"

"You are *not* my mother, Kate," Marcus chuckled. "You're just a gold digger than thinks she's hit the jackpot. But that stops... now."

Kate exploded. "That's it, you little bastard. You're cut off. I'm the executor of the estate, which means you get nothing until I say you do, or until I die. *That's* the way it works. And *now*, you little shit, I'll be damn sure there's not a penny left when I go."

Marcus laughed. "Then I'd start spending if I were you... quickly."

Kate was livid, chain-eating the candies, as she got angrier. "You get your ass out of this house right now, or I'll have Bobby toss you out on your well-pampered ass."

Marcus laughed again and stood. "Actually I was thinking of staying the weekend, since I'll be moving into the master suite."

"Bobby... get your ass in here!" Kate shouted, glaring at Marcus.

The patio door opened and Bobby Hanson walked in, all six feet six inches of blond hair and suntan of him. Bobby was Kate's driver... in more ways than one, Marcus knew. He put his hand on Marcus's shoulder and squeezed tightly. "You giving your mom shit, asshole?"

Marcus cocked his head at Kate and winked, a placid smile forming on his face.

It was over in a few seconds. Bobby suddenly found his hand locked in a painful grasp. Then they both spun around as Marcus rotated his arm and drove his knee hard into Bobby's crotch. A quick reversal drove his heel in to the back of the body builder's knees and with a loud *pop* Bobby found himself kneeling much like he was at prayer, facing Kate, one arm wedged behind him. Without taking his eyes from his stepmother's, Marcus calmly took the Colt Commander from his belt holster, placed it to the base of Bobby's skull and blew his brains out, letting the body drop to the floor.

"She is *not* my mother."

Kate opened her mouth to scream when the first shooting pain hit her behind the eyes and the floor went sideways, dropping her back into the large armchair.

Marcus sat back down. "Is there a problem, Kate?"

Kate tried to speak, but her face felt numb and uncontrolled.

"Oh, that. That's what is commonly called a stroke, Kate, and a pretty bad one, by the looks of it."

He stood and carefully picked up the goblet, popping a peppermint into his mouth. His stepmother looked back and forth from him to the candies. "Oh, these? Absolutely poisoned. A derivative of curare I tweaked a bit. They're completely blood pressure triggered. Stay calm and the poison passes through your system in a matter of hours. But go too high, and *bang,* stroke-like symptoms. The more you ingest, the more severe the effect, and, since you've been eating them like they've been going out of style for the last ten minutes now, I'd say this is as good as it gets."

Marcus stood up and stepped over to kiss his step-mom on the forehead. "But don't worry. I am a dutiful son, after all. Everyone says so. I'll make sure you get the best care. Nurses and staff, a nice room in the guest wing with a sunny patio, 'round the clock care." He kneeled down close to her ear. "But one of these nights, sometime down the road, I'm going to come in and strangle you very slowly until you pass on into the next life. It could be tonight. It could be ten years from now. You'll have plenty of time to think about that, I bet. Now, if you'll excuse me, I have a call to make."

Marcus picked up the phone and dialed a number. "Hello, Mister Mand, please. Tell him that Dr. Marcus Jamison is calling about his offer."

Cave

"Sir," Dietrich said, wiping the sweat from his forehead, the hot Indian sun beating down mercilessly. "Are you sure this is the location?"

Marcus nodded, directing the Hindi workers to continue digging. "I'm sure. This is where She told me to dig, and She has never been wrong in the past."

The ex-SS commando shrugged. "If you say so, sir. It just seems a bit… remote."

"As it would be, my friend. They were secretive with their temples. Had to be with the British hunting them down day and night. The texts that I've researched say that they often left the less competent members to carry out random acts of violence just so the Brits would think they were annihilating them, while they built strongholds in the surrounding wilderness."

As they spoke, a commotion started over by the dig site, and Dietrich checked on it. "They say they found something, sir."

Marcus made his way over to the pit. At its floor, some buried masonry had given away to reveal a deep dark hole that led deeper into the ground. "I'll need a vertical drop kit and a lantern, quickly." Marcus quickly donned a climbing harness. "Lower me down if you would, Dietrich." Fifty feet or so later, Marcus's booted feet touched ground, the lantern illuminating the antechamber. He marveled for a moment at the painted walls and detailed sculptures. "They never found you here, did they my friends?" he said to the kneeling skeletons about the chambers.

Stepping back into sight of the fissure, he called up, "This is it, Dietrich. You and your men may commence." As he probed deeper into the caves, he could hear the automatic fire echo from above. Light came through carefully constructed ventilation holes hundreds of years old, drawing fresh air down into the outer chambers, while the inner one remained sealed. A few ventilation fans would be all he needed to purge the foul air that more than likely awaited in the inner chambers.

Footsteps heralded Dietrich's entrance into the antechamber of the temple. "Everything is as expected, sir?"

Marcus nodded, "Absolutely, my friend."

Dietrich began to distribute the various supply and equipment cases as they were lowered down, enough supplies for six months alone. After a little searching, Marcus found a hidden cistern, which when tested proved to be more than pure enough to drink.

Finally, the set up was complete and Dietrich prepared to be lifted from the chamber. "Is there anything else you need, sir?"

Marcus thought for a moment, and then checked a case. "Nope... plenty of hash and wine, I think I'll be fine."

Dietrich chuckled, "Then I will see you in six months?"

Marcus nodded.

"Stay ahead of that *swinehund*, Mand, Marcus. He will come looking, sooner or later."

"And if he's stupid enough to come here, I do believe he'll find more of what the British found," Marcus replied casually, gesturing to the pile of skeletons, bits of British colonial forces uniforms still clinging to them. "And *they* didn't have claymore mines."

With a nod, Dietrich ascended the ropes and, with the help of his mercenaries, eased the cover stone back over the entrance, leaving Marcus alone with the dead.

And his Goddess.

"I'm here, Mistress. Teach me what you will," Marcus whispered as he began to crack the seals on the inner chambers.

I will, my love, the voice replied. *I will show you everything.*

Exhumed

Todd Oliver hated clearing projects with a passion, especially almost forty year-old foundations. You never knew when there would be a sub-basement or crawlway that would suddenly make itself known… like this one had just done. Of course, it did not help his mood that he was laying on his back, looking up at the sky through the hole about ten feet above him.

"Hey, Todd, you ok?" the foreman yelled down.

"Yeah, I'm fine, just get a damn ladder, ok?" Todd grumbled as he stood and dusted himself off. "Oh… toss me a light. Might as well look around while I'm here."

The foreman laughed, and dropped a Mag-Light down to him. Flicking it on, Todd looked around. The nearest end was all rubble where the foundation had collapsed and settled, but the other end seemed to be heavily reinforced.

"Hmmm… they said there was a church or something here, wonder if an alter or something was above it."

Low on the reinforced wall, there was a steel door, about four feet high, like the ones he had seen on old bomb shelters. There was no visible lock or anything on it, and after a few tries Todd finally forced the handle with the rugged flashlight. The air huffed out and Todd covered his face with his sleeve in case he caught a whiff of gas. Nothing smelled foul, so he shined his flashlight into the space beyond, and almost dropped it.

"Holy Shit," he said as he stepped back under the hole. "Dude, get an ambulance and Pinnacle PD. You are *NOT* gonna believe this!"

Rewind...

War

Gunfire sounded about the compound as Incense burst into the office. "We are in some serious shit, my love. The Liberty League just showed up."

Peppermint turned to the twins, Yin and Mai, handing each a small package and opened the secret tunnel in the floor. "Quickly now, my special ones, fast and silent -- it is not your day to die. You must make sure these items get to the proper people in the Blackguard Isles."

The young Japanese twins bowed low and then each kissed his cheek. "We love you, master. Die well." Then they disappeared down the tunnels and into the sewers of Pinnacle City. Peppermint closed the hatch, counted to twenty and pressed the detonator, sealing the tunnel behind his twin couriers.

"Darling, we might have had a use for that tunnel." Incense joked as she reloaded her Skorpion machine pistols.

"But, luv, we still have *sooo* much to do." He glanced at the monitors, currently displaying the newly formed Independence Corps operatives forcing their way through the makeshift barriers his followers had set up earlier. And behind them he could see Patrioteer and his Liberty League.

"Lovely." he frowned. "He's early."

Incense quipped, "So much for existential time travel, love."

"Hardly. This is a special case, luv. After all, he has some help in making his future slippery to see. And just knowing the future can affect it, we've been over that." Peppermint zipped up his fighting suit and made sure his brace of kris-bladed daggers was seated along his shoulder blade where he could reach them quickly. Hefting the old Stoner 63a Commando/M-203 combo with its blue under-slung 100-round drum magazine of 5.56mm Nato he started for the door.

Incense raised an eyebrow. "You're bringing the Cookie Monster? It *must* be bad."

Peppermint just chuckled and stepped out into the hallway, the amassed Church members parting like a sea as their Godhead walked among them. With a flip of a hidden switch, various walls slid open all over the compound, each revealing a plethora of small arms. Peppermint pickup up a hidden mike and keyed it on.

"The war is upon us, my children. The closed-minded are at the gate. It is time, children, to rise up and defend this place – your place!" Cheers echoed as weapons were distributed by acolytes of the church to any member strong enough to pick them up. Men, women, even children boiled out into the compound and opened fire on the surprised law enforcement agents. The hail of fire on the monitors was staggering.

"My God, Marcus… how 'deep in them' are you?" Incense asked, shock leaking into the assassin's voice. She knew that Marcus Jamison was a master of manipulation. The Church of the Poison Mind had drained millions from its members to fund its secondary operations, but until now she had always thought the cult was an affectation, a way to bleed money out of its patrons and into the compound to build up rep and fund the various drug and sex rackets. The shock was doubled when he suddenly slapped her.

"Mother of Darkness, not is *not* the time for blasphemy," he said as he keyed the intercom to another channel, this one to the PA system, *Beethoven's Sixth Symphony* suddenly blaring from the speakers set all over the compound.

"Everyone, *hear* me: Clockwork Lemon!"

Incense was just about to cold-cock Marcus when she saw several groups of the older soldiers and law enforcement agents suddenly turn on their own. "What? How?"

Marcus chuckled, "You have to love Mand. Never wasted an asset. Now, we have to get to the temple."

Incense grinned. "Lets rock and roll, then, my love." The pair launched out into the courtyard, guns blazing as they headed through the chaos and toward the center structure of the compound.

Court

"The court finds the defendant, Marcus Jamison, unable to stand trial in his current state."

The courtroom exploded into a cacophony of murmurs, and the judge banged his gavel repeatedly for the din to quiet. Then one voice boomed out, clear and loud over all the others as Patrioteer stood. "You will explain yourself!"

Sister Starchild put her head in her hand, muttering "Oh, hell."

Judge Collins pointed his gavel at Patrioteer. "In light of your contributions to this city over the decades, I will choose *not* to hold you in contempt of court, provided you sit down *now*, Patrioteer. I am aware of your investment on this case, and I will explain my decision."

"Marcus Jamison, a/k/a 'Dr. Peppermint' is, to put it very simply, a vegetable. There is no consciousness to charge, no guilt to determine, no plea to enter. His mind is gone, proven through a battery of examinations including those by your own psychic associate, Sister Starchild. If he cannot understand the charges and cannot participate in his defense, then he simply cannot stand trial."

Patrioteer's eyes flared. "With all due respect, your Honor, something must be done. Over two hundred and fifty people died that day at the assault on his compound in 1975, and many of the survivors are still in therapy for the teachings this lunatic conducted. He had women – *children* – armed with assault weapons and firing on police and agents of a half-dozen federal agencies. Not to mention that he was running a murder-for-hire association under the guise of that abhorrent church *and* an offshoot of the Thuggie cult!"

"Patrioteer, that is all conjecture. I am charged with the duty to determine guilt and consequences by what we know, what can be proven through evidence and witnesses. In this case, there are no competent witnesses that the defendant was directly responsible for the actions of his followers in response to the attack on the Church of the Purified Mind-"

"Poison Mind," Patrioteer interrupted. Collins locked him with a steely gaze.

"No document recovered utilizes that name, sir. And any evidence of this cult was buried under tons of rubble when *you* leveled the place. *Technically,* you should be serving time right now for *your* actions in the disaster."

"Excuse me?" Patrioteer looked stunned.

"Federal Agents were warranted and approved only to seize financial records for alleged tax evasion-"

"An allegation later proven unsubstantiated, I might add," Jamison's attorney interjected, then shrank in his seat under the withering glare of Patrioteer.

"As I was saying. This seizure was backed by Independence Corps agents that you *insisted* be there. Agents, I might add, that opened fire on the crowd first."

"They were being manipulated psychically!" Patrioteer objected.

"Again, there no witness to that fact, but *several hundred* witnesses say they were defending themselves from Independence Corps, some of which even opened fire on law enforcement officers who were trying to shut down the riot!"

"They were from Jamison's unit in Vietnam," Patrioteer countered, disbelief that the judge was not seeing the whole picture adding to his frenzy.

"Jamison was a MASH field psychologist during Vietnam."

"He was a CIA operator and interrogator," Patrioteer vehemently countered.

The judge had had enough, and slammed the hefty file down on his desk.

"Where is the *proof*? There is *no* record that Dr. Jamison was anything more than a field physician; *no* connection to the CIA; *no* connection to some fabled assassination team, and born roughly three hundred years too late to belong to any Thuggie cult, which, by the way, was eradicated in the 1800s by the British Empire as I recall." The judge was dangerously close to rising from his chair, leaning heavily upon his desk.

"But…"

"Not another word, or I *will* hold you in contempt of court, 'city savoir' or no."

Sister Starchild reached up and placed a light hand on Patrioteer's arm. "Please, it's over. Let it go."

Patrioteer paused for a moment, then took a deep breath and let it out slowly. "Fine…*your honor*… perhaps he's covered himself and the atrocities he committed. But he will not stay free, so say I!"

"No, he will not. My judgment is that Marcus Jamison will be remanded to the custody of the Maximum Security Medical Wing of Kennedy Penitentiary until such time as he can stand trial."

Patrioteer turned and looked at the catatonic Marcus Jamison. "And *I* will be waiting for that day."

        "And you" Judge Collins pointed his gavel at Patrioteer "are in contempt of this court. Remain in this courtroom until such time as I determine your sentence."

Rewind…

Pinnacle

His arms spread wide, he stood on the ledge of the building, his *rumal* clutched in one hand like a ghastly banner of victory, looking down over Promethium Park, the Delphi-laced peppermints hitting his system like a freight train, forcing his third eye open wide to the spheres. Screams filtered up from the streets as the survivors ran, trying to escape the multiple explosions that rang out across the city. Sporadically, another hijacked Warp Corp dimensional portal would open to eject another Fuel Air Bomb or launch another gas canister filled with Vishnu or Morrigan into the crowds to bring another wave of drug-induced civil chaos for Thunderbolt to deal with.

Behind him, the young acolyte stood up. "It's rigged… whenever you're ready, Master."

He stepped away from the edge, smiling, and walked over to her.

"My dear, Chrysanthemum, as I have said before: there are no Masters, only Teachers and Students, and even those are one and the same."

She passed him and he leaned down so she could place a kiss on his cheek. "I love you, Teacher. I will see you again." Without another word she disrobed and dove from the building's edge toward the concrete a hundred stories below, the C-4 vest detonating on impact, sending thousands of ball bearings flying at the speed of sound through the PCPD storming the building.

Marcus knelt and looked over the control panel

for a moment, then keyed the detonator, counting down from thirty seconds. He returned to the ledge of the building and smiled, whispering to the burning skies. The words barely left his lips when he felt the impact of the detonation of the stolen alien Skree Domination "City-Killer" device.

"The way is ready, my Love, my Teacher, My Mother… step through."

The world exploded into white light, and then darkness.

Incense and Peppermint

The heavy walls of the central building of the Compound muted the gunfire as Dr. Peppermint closed the doors to the main hall. There gathered, uniformed in their various chosen fighting suits, was the core of the Church of the Poison Mind: seventy-five assassins and zealous devotees to Dr. Peppermint. He smiled as they came to him, touching him as a child would touch a parent… as a follower would touch a messiah.

"Now, my students, is the greatest lesson of all. It is the time of reckoning, and the time for you to gather all you can for the Mother of Night. The Enemy is gathered outside these walls. And it is your duty to bring the Good Death to our children, and the Bad Death to our foes." He lit a brazier, and withdrew from the base a small block wrapped in tin foil. As he opened it, Incense's heightened senses picked out the scent immediately. Hashish. He dropped the entire kilo into the brazier.

"Breathe deeply, my Students and open your *third eye*… your Mistress calls to you to do her bidding. Her arms are open wide." The assassins did as they were told, chanting in a dozen different tongues praises to Peppermint's goddess, to Kali, the Mother of Night.

"Now, go!"

The drugged zealots exploded into action, weapons drawn, as they exited the temple to flow into the bedlam outside in twos and threes, dispatching foes with blade, fist, gun and with *rumal* for those deserving. Once the last had gone, Peppermint locked a top over the brazier and kicked on an exhaust fan. After a moment, Incense released the breath she had been holding.

"I wish you'd warn me when you do stuff like that."

Peppermint wrinkled his nose. "I know it's supposed to be tradition, but to tell you the truth I could never get a taste for the stuff. Never did anything more than stink up the room and give me the munchies," he confided, taking a few peppermint swirls from a bowl and popping them in his mouth to cut the taste of the thick black drug.

Incense sneezed several times in succession. "Well, I almost got a lung-full of that crap."

Peppermint chuckled. "My dear, that's been soaking in Vishnu for months, you might have enjoyed it. Then again, you may have also fucked yourself to death with all those strapping young soldiers out there." He added as an afterthought.

"Funny man." she said. "Now what?"

"Now we wait for him, and when he comes for me, I kill him."

"Him. You mean Patrioteer, don't you?"

"Astute as always, my love." He began to undress. "The children are almost done, are you ready?"

Incense stripped off the cinnamon and red Kevlar-weave body suit. "This may not be the weirdest thing you've ever talked me into doing, but it ranks up there, you know?"

"It's tantric, my love, the strongest energy, and with your bloodline, you're the biggest D-cell I could find." He laughed and donned black silk pants, the striped *rumal* around his neck like a scarf. "And as to the weirdest thing I've ever talked you into, I recall a weekend in Bangladesh…"

"You made it sound so romantic, and it was your birthday, ass!" She laughed as she interrupted him. He caressed her flesh, one hand drifting between her legs.

"And there was that time in Studio 54's bathroom."

"Ugh, don't remind me." Her eyes opened wide as Marcus did something out of her range of sight. *"Holy crap*, what the hell was that?"

"Just some special oils, luv," he guided her, repositioning her on her hands and knees in front of him. "All part of the process."

Incense looked over her shoulder, "Well, warn a girl, would ya… It feels like you've hooked my pelvis up to house current."

Peppermint made himself ready as the sounds of gunfire drew near. They were in the building. Not long now. He entered her slowly, and her breath caught in her throat. "Om… my god… wow… jesopete. What the hell are you doing to me?" Incense had always known that Marcus was one of the most attentive lovers she had had, something to do with all the yoga and breathing shit, she figured, but now, she suddenly could not keep herself propped up, and with each thrust waves built within her, feelings she had never experienced. Incense imagined that this must be what a champagne bottle feels like right before the cork goes flying.

The sounds of gunfire seemed to come from right outside the door, as Marcus began to speed up his rhythm. The vibrations building within her began to grow beyond anything she had ever felt before, making her want it to both end and go on forever.

"Marcus... I... I... I'm not going to be able to do... this... much... longer."

"Almost there, luv," Marcus's voice was a hissing whisper, the power building in the pit of his stomach. "Allllmost therrrrrre."

"Oh... Oh... Oh Shit... OH MY FUCKING GOD... WHY CAN'T I...I NEED TOO... I NEED TOOOOO..."

Marcus aligned his chakras, and drew his right hand back in a spear point.

"Now, my sweet. Now." He exhaled slowly.

Incense felt the release explode inside her, through her, and in that instant Indera Kalammni existed everywhere and nowhere at once.

She never felt the blow that ended her life.

Pause…

Time Travel

"But didn't you die in 1980?"

John Lennon laughed. "You know as well as I do, Marcus, there's no death without rebirth. And, anyway, it's 1970."

Marcus finished his martini, and smiled at Twiggy as she cruised by. "So, then it's true. Time is simply a perceptual state."

John refilled the martini glass. "That's what Paul and I were trying to tell everyone, but they all just kept hearing, 'Paul is dead.' Bloody stupid gits, they are. Ah, look who's here."

Marcus turned toward where Lennon was gesturing, and saw her dancing. "Indera." He started to move, but John stopped him.

"Sorry, luv, but its March tenth, and you're still in Barni, India, in the enforced coma, remember?"

Marcus winced, remembering the "sabbatical" that Mand had him take, and what the CIA had pulled while he was there. If it was March, then Dietrich would not even be extracting him for another month, and then he'd still have to find the cave…

"It takes some getting used to, John," Marcus chuckled, taking another sip.

"That it does, mate, but you get the hang of it after a while. Just do what I do: have another drink and enjoy the ride," Lennon replied, laughing.

"Now, let me ask you something, Marcus. Is that no-talent bitch still making money off me name?"

Patrioteer

The Independence Corps soldiers kicked through the door in time to see their target nearly take his lover's head off with a single blow, their weapons leveled and ready to fire.

They never had a chance.

Peppermint threw his head back with a yell and leapt forward over Indera's body, his face covered with face paint like a red-pink colored skull, landing before them. He screamed a single word that their minds could not comprehend and men dropped like puppets with their strings cut, thick blood leaking from their eyes, ears, and nose. Peppermint stalked past the bodies and out into hell, his eyes searching through the smoke for his target.

Patrioteer barely heard the Spirit of Patriots' warning echo in his head, when the weight hit him from behind driving him to the ground. He spun as another blow smashed him off his feet and through a light pylon. Marcus Jamison floated three feet above the ground, dark tendrils swirling about him. Something in Patrioteer's gut twisted. There was something *more* here. Then the Spirit of Patriots confirmed it in one word he had never heard her say to him.

Run!

He stood, and Jamison was on him. Never had he fought someone like this before. He was everywhere at once, the blows taking bites out of his soul. Each one that landed seemed to dim the spark of America a bit. He struck out, blindly, and connected, hurling Jamison away from him. *Spirit… what is this man*?

The reply came as through static, and he could see Jamison's lips move with the voice of the Patriots within his head:

I am become Shiva, destroyer of worlds.

He shook his head and Jamison was on him again, the blue and white striped silk scarf tightening around his neck. Patrioteer would have laughed at the attack any other time, but he found himself without breath; the sacred *rumal*, the scarf-weapon of the ancient Strangler Cult, crushing his windpipe, drawing his very life from him. His sight grew dim… *This cannot be happening!*

Suddenly the weight was lifted from him. A steel hand threw Jamison away from him.   Multiple punches rained down on Jamison staggering him. As the metal-sheathed giant helped Patrioteer up, he felt he should know these people somehow. Then he saw *himself* fly at Jamison, smashing him from the sky with powerful fists… his fists.

As Jamison began to stagger to his feet, a gorgeous platinum blond with café-au-let skin stepped from the smoke and locked her eyes on Jamison, the psychic force almost tangible. Then, incredibly, Jamison struggled to one knee. "He's strong. I'm… I'm not sure I can hold him. He's getting help from somewhere. I think I can- OH MY GOD!" Fear crossed over her beautiful face. "Patrioteer… stop him, please… stop him… SHE'S COMING THROUGH!"

Patrioteer launched without thinking, smashing with all his strength into Jamison, the other "him" following up, working in concert. Jamison was smashed back into the temple and then the other brought down the entire structure. As the temple collapsed, he caught a glimpse in the dark sky of something *wrong,* then it vanished as the group of heroes leveled the temple.

As he got to his feet, he looked at his other self, who simply winked and vanished into the smoke. The blond "star child" lingered for a moment longer.

"Never let him win, Patrioteer. Never."

Her words faded as Patrioteer looked around at the devastation all around him. In his ears he heard the disturbing man-woman-chorus voice echoing as his breath caught in his throat.

"I am become Shiva, destroyer of worlds."

Cycle

As the news reporter droned on about the terrorist attacks that all but leveled Pinnacle City, Jane Haddon smiled up at her husband painfully as the paramedics wheeled her gurney into the delivery room.

"I think one of the twins just kicked…"

Dr. Peppermint will return...

Eden Succeeding

by Christopher L. DelGuercio

Prologue

I am the Meatman, and I bring them the meat.

I've served three masters in my life. As I speak to you now, I am The Chronicler of Events because I'm the only one left who can perform the task, but when we originally landed on Second Eden, I was to be an Instructor of Knowledges—my formal training. An instructor for a generation that we soon came to realize would never bloom here. A dead end job if ever there was one.

It was then that I discovered my true calling. My people wanted meat, and I provided it. I was good at it. I did it willingly. I made no apologies then, nor do I now.

I am The Meatman. I bring them the meat.

BEFORE THE FALL

1

Mud covered my legs and a suction *pop* of air exploded with each step I pulled out of the muck. It was always like this on Eden after a rain. And there was always a rain. I trudged through it all, my squat body hunched close to the ground, weighted down by an arsenal of edged metals. It was an efficient way for a man like me to travel without the benefit of wide siltshoes to keep my feet aboveground: a slow-rolling waddle, shuffling, the way a drootmunk moves. Besides, when Bean's deformed feet punched through the wiring of his own shoes, I gave the boy mine. He needed them, being too spindly and sick to drootwalk.

"Keep up," I called out to the boy, forgetting Eden's influence had not only slowed his feet but the sound of my voice was becoming lost to him as well. His ears had withered and dropped off, and their canals had narrowed. The growth of shingles over the holes forced Bean to rely on the reading of my lips, but he was not always successful with the wire-tangle of beard I had hanging over my mouth and creeping across my face. I waved him forward and watched him double-time it to catch me. Trotting alongside me now, he labored for breath.

We were still within the safety of the outer bushwoods, a hedgerow of deep, wild greenery sitting atop a mesh of subterranean roots, so I slowed my gait and the two of us began to walk. I took out my journal and surveyed the clear sky of Eden's phytoplankton-rich atmosphere, olive green at the horizon and darkening as my gaze went up. Its pale sun blazed down on us. Bean turned his head to face me, his neck ratcheting loudly, each diseased click of his vertebrae sickening me to my core. I tried like hell to disguise my groan, but failed. I hastily finished my entry and returned the journal to my coat pocket.

"I don't think I should work for you anymore," he said, his dull, gray eyes raised to meet my healthy blues. He was slapping at the leaves and the plump turquoise fruit hanging from the branches of the jimp trees to our right. "It's useless. I'm only slowing you down anyway."

I remember when he first came to me two years ago, his eyes had held such warmth. They'd been a deep brown, so soft they looked like a pelt. I would never forget those eyes. Never. The boy was right, of course. I didn't want him to know that, but my silence said as much.

"For godsakes, why do you even still take me with you?" he continued, a defiance I'd never heard from him before ringing in his voice, almost as if his approaching end served to strengthen him. It made me proud in a strange way.

"I know why my father asked you to take me on," he said. "But it's clearly not working; I'm not like you. Eden's already too much inside me."

It was good to see someone share in my anger. "What makes you so sure we're not alike?" I asked.

"Just look at me!" His voice strained and cracked. He massaged his neck, the verdant skin alive with bulging, pulsing rivulets of vein. "You want me to say it? You want to hear me say I'm a goner?" I shook my head. "I'm not like you at all."

I grabbed hold of his arms. "People believe their eyes," I told him. "But their eyes only tell them what they already believe."

I could see that he was shocked that I grabbed him. "What do you mean?" he said.

"*You* can't even see it, with all the time you

spend with me." I gave a half-hearted laugh. "I'm dying like all the rest." I let go of him and yanked at my sleeve to reveal a hairy, muscled forearm. Dark dirt encrusted my hands, framing each fingernail. I turned my palm up and while my hand was a permanent black, the inside of my arm was clean and covered with scars that wound up and down the length of me like pink worms.

Bean's eyes got wide. "Are those from the lissur?"

I nodded. "Those first years as Meatman I found out I'd wear my mistakes for the rest of my life. But that's not what I want you to see." I thrust my arm into the boy's face. "Look closer."

Bean examined the skin carefully. "You're jaundiced," he said with surprise.

I nodded again and rolled down my sleeve. "After that, I'll green, and then brown and harden." I squared up my face with his. "Do you see my eyes?"

The boy squinted and narrowed his eyes to chalk-colored slits.

"You see the snow in them?"

"All I see is blue," Bean said.

"Believe me, there's white in there too. It won't be long before they're as silver as yours. No one's getting spared, my friend. It just feels that way to you because you're farther along. We're all riding on the same train, just in different cars. Just one track though."

He seemed to take the news of our shared fates with genuine cheer, even fighting back a grin. I allowed him that. It was damn hard being a kid in this place, and no one—kid or not—wants to feel like they're alone in this, or any, world. We walked on beneath the harsh stare of Eden's sun, feeling a little better that we'd gotten a scream or two out of our systems.

"You know I was scared when father told me I was apprenticing with you," Bean said.

A smile rose up on my face. "Am I so scary to you first gens?"

"My friends all say you're some kind of a witch, charming the dirt dragons and cooking up secret potions, just you and Nessa all alone in the bush."

"Warlock," I said. "A woman is a witch but a man's called a warlock." I had to chuckle. "So is that really what they say about me?"

"Oh yeah, and that's not all. I didn't know if I was more frightened of the lissur or you." His voice still held some innocence. The child inside that decayed husk glimmered through for just a moment and his words held this dumb, bittersweet smile clinging to me.

"How old are you now, Bean?"

"Thirteen," he said, puffing out his chest slightly. "What about you? I bet you're really old, huh?"

"Hey, I'm only thirty-eight," I told him.

"Yeah, that's really old."

I shrugged. When most first gens didn't see their tenth birthday, thirteen must have felt positively elderly, and I must've looked like Methuselah. In the deep distance, clouds coalesced. "We'd better pick it up. We've got redfields to cross and there's another storm coming." I sank my feet into the mud again.

The boy nodded and quickened his pace. "You talk like my dad sometimes. Were you ever someone's dad, back on Earth?"

"Nope," I said. "Me and Nessa, we didn't want to raise any children back there."

"So you were waiting until you got to Eden?"

I paused a moment before I took another step. "That was our big plan, all right. But you know what they say about the best-laid plans of mice and men."

"The best-laid what?"

"No, I guess you wouldn't, would you?" I said. "Probably better that way."

Bean shook at my arm playfully. "Okay, as usual I'm totally lost right now. So tell me what happened," he said, "with you and Nessa. And stop looking so gloomy, I'm the one who's sick, remember?"

"Maybe you should concentrate on keeping pace instead of talking so much," I said.

"I'm sorry. I'm always prying, that's what father says." Bean clammed up and kept moving.

But after a while his sullenness got to eating at my gut. I was feeling guilty. After two years with me I guess the boy did deserve something more than I was giving him. But how could I make him understand that we couldn't bring children into this world either? I finally blurted out the words.

"Did *you* like growing up here?"

He smiled, pleased our conversation hadn't ended, paused in thought for a moment, then spoke. "I remember my mom would read me stories and sing to me in bed. I used to love that. Me and my dad would play catch with garva nuts. And, oh, thanks to you my baby brother thinks I'm a medieval knight or something." He stretched his arms out. "Yeah, I even had a girlfriend once." He had the far-off look of an older man reminiscing over a spent lifetime. "It's been better than not growing up at all," he said.

Christ on a crutch, what could I say to that? Damn this kid! I've never heard anyone be so thankful for so little. I guess after almost forty years breathing—half of them spent with the woman I love—I don't get to feel sorry for myself.

"If I'm being honest, this place scared us," I told him. "We couldn't fathom bringing a child up in this place, same as the last one. Maybe we're cowards."

Bean shook his head vigorously. "You're the bravest person I know."

I placed my hand on top of the boy's head. "If we knew then that having a kid like you was even possible, I think we might have changed our minds."

He reached up and wrapped his arm around my shoulder as we walked and my feet seemed to lighten. I imagine this must be what it feels like to have a son of your own. I have to remember to put this is my journal.

But the next moment my thoughts wandered to Nessa and the inevitability of the time we had left together. I wanted to tell Bean how my chest tightened every time I took out that creased and faded picture of her at the lake, looking the way she used to. I wanted to explain to him that I couldn't accept my life here, or anywhere else, without her. I wanted to say that I was jealous of Eden, how its grip held increasing sway over her. But he's just a kid, with plenty of his own lamentations. No sense in piling mine on him too. There would be no children for Nessa and I.

"It's too late now," was all I told him. "That's all there is to it."

2

After galumphing through the strangling brush, we brought our feet down onto a blue-green forest bed, and soon after, emerged at the clearing where my thatched-roof house stood. We passed the white blossoms of the almond tree Nessa and I planted when we first put down stakes and walked to the door I fashioned myself from twistwood all those years before. I laid the day's catch into a barrow and told Bean, "Wheel this around back to the chop house." Then lifting the lever, I pressed my weight against the heavy wooden door.

Nessa's croaking voice called to me from the bedroom. "Is that you, Jon?" She vomited the words out as if they were glass shards. The sound grated against my ears.

From the barrel beside the door, I ladled a jug full of water and brought it to the bedroom. Yellowed photographs, half-covered with a sheet and speckled with mold, cluttered the dresser where her jewelry box stood. I placed the jug beside the bed and untied the harnesses that held her wrists to the bedposts, carefully avoiding the wide pink channels where the bindings had gouged through the toughened skin of her arms. With any lingering shred of strength I possessed, I hoisted her upright on the bed.

Her skin was brown and striated. She snatched the jug from my hands and poured the water down her gullet, letting it spill down her sides. With great zeal, she rubbed the overflow over her leathery flesh.

"How was today?" I asked gently.

"I dreamed," she said between gulps of water.

"Is that good?"

"I dreamed that I was this enormous thing." She spread her arms as far as they would stretch and the water sloshed in the jug. "An enormous, *living thing*, or at least I think I was."

Each new vision Eden presented to her terrified me more than the last. "And you're big?" I asked.

"It's not just that I'm big—it's *how* I'm big. I'm all middle." She screwed her face up. "I'm this greasy, pulsing thing—like an egg sack. It sounds scary, right?"

I nodded.

"Do you know what the scariest part about it was? I don't think it was a dream at all."

"Please, Nessa, don't. It was just a dream." A rock formed in my throat. "Don't say that. You know it kills me when you—"

"I heard the voices, too," she said, not listening to me anymore.

"The voices are lies, Nessa. We've been over this." I touched her hair, softly, for fear of it coming loose in my hand. Most of it had discolored and fallen out already, but there were still patches with roots strong enough to allow a calloused, roughhewn palm like mine to slide over them. "I'm sorry I wasn't home sooner," I told her. "I could've helped you make sense of this."

She looked at me, but I avoided her pupil-less eyes. Instead, I caressed her cheek with my palm and felt the rigidity that had taken over her entire body. She was hard, like a corpse, and instinctively I drew my hand away. Nessa's face sagged as if she were about to cry, but we both knew no tears would come from these new eyes. She trembled as I held her close and my eyes wept, doing the work for both of us.

"But the voices," she said. "They don't feel like lies."

I pulled away then rubbed at my temples. "They… are… lies! Don't listen to them," I said. "Bean's in the back. There's meat that needs tending. I'll be a while."

"You'll be here, just out back?" she said. "Then you don't have to use the straps on me this time. I promise I won't leave."

"Okay then," I said as I made for the door. I opened it and stopped there with my back to her. How could I be mad? None of this was her fault. I turned around. "I need you," I said.

She smiled and poured the last of the water into a cup. "Thank you, Jon. You're so sweet to me." I left her in our bedroom and exited the front door. From the outside, I bolted it shut.

I walked over the fallen almond blossoms around back to the small shed I'd built when I first took up hunting—nothing more than a single-room hut with vertical slats set apart for air to flow through, like a gap-toothed smile. At the doorway, I took out my journal and scribbled a few passages in it.

Bean was already elbow-deep in the basin tub, chopping the meat into manageable pieces. He threw each slab into the tub with a wet *thwap*. I pulled a carafe of berrystain from a crowded shelf of variegated bottles and poured the crimson liquid over the meat. Opaque, clay jars of plant and seed oil extracts, a mortar and pestle, and spice vials were all nearby on the shelves. I stretched out my hands and my fingers made an audible *crack*.

The creator's time was at hand.

The preparation of the meat was sacrament. I dyed it in a mixture primarily made of the juice from a common local berry, which transformed the meat's previous mud-color into a deadflesh scarlet. Once the meat was removed from the tub, the juice sweated out, leaving a deceptively grisly shadow on the cutting board. The berry itself was the blandest sort and offered no clue that the *juices* within the meat were anything but the sweet lifeblood of an animal everyone knew didn't exist on Second Eden.

This sight alone brought most of the Alpha settlement out of their caves and hovels on the day of the market, but providing mere sustenance was never enough for me. I was an artisan, a true virtuoso, a painter who worked in the medium of the senses. A magician, but of the best kind because my legerdemain made mouths water and brought forth memories of home. So as countless hours and days here strung together into countless months and years, I collected a mixture of tastes, scents, and textures that would mimic a small piece of what we'd left behind on Earth. And the lissur provided the perfect canvas. This quaggy, utterly tasteless meat would be at the heart of each of my little masterpieces.

There were minute differences from beef, to be certain. The lingering pungency from the soil that encapsulated these beasts their entire lives— centuries, millennia even, how were we to know. Then there was the meat's consistency—softer, more like that of a scallop than of cattle. Even the dying solution itself, with the slightest hint of citrus, could serve to reveal my ruse. But it never did. Because the most powerful seasoning of all was one I didn't have to add: The homesick mind. Any imperfect flavor or aroma, any sensation missing or untrue was masked by the customers making them, ultimately, the final chef.

No one knew—I don't think they even cared to

know—how I did what I did. They knew only that I faced the monsters for them.

I was The Meatman, and I'd bring them their meat.

In the final stages of preparation, after brining the day's catch and applying a spice rub I concocted from jerk root and pepris, I wrapped the lot in sunsplash leaves to preserve them for the long trip to market. Our sojourn was tomorrow and my task was now complete. Red up to my elbows in berrystain and stinking of wormy flesh, I came back into the house.

"Is the meat ready?" Nessa asked. She sounded better. The water had soothed the coarseness in her voice and her short-lived freedom to move about the house had nourished her spirit.

I took her by the hand but felt nothing of the woman I loved remaining in its stiff, cool grip. "Me and the boy are leaving for market."

"So soon? I wish you could stay a while longer. You spend more time with that meat than you do with me."

"The meat is our life, Nessa. You know that."

Her head drooped as far as the disease would let it. "You want me back on the bed, don't you?"

"You're sick," I said. "I can't have you just wandering off to the bush. We both know what happens when Eden gets inside you."

She squeezed her hand out of mine. "I won't listen to the voices, I swear. I'll stay right here in the house. I won't—"

"No!" My voice was more of a howl than I'd intended. "I'm sorry. But no."

She slunk quietly into bed and lifted her arms into the straps. I fastened her right hand in and tightened it. I couldn't bear to lose her. I needed her that much, even though I couldn't trust her not to be seduced by Eden's voices.

Was that still love?

I can't tell anymore, but it didn't stop me from tightening the strap around her left hand as well.

3

A clearing existed on our sliver of Eden, where the planet's crust itself seemed to have grown out of the ground to shape a great hall of sorts. The crag, flattened smooth from constant weathering, poked up from beneath the soil, creating stone tables. The entire field was floored in this same stone. Under the wan light of dawn, vendors marched into the clearing from all directions, flashing between the shadows, and then popping out suddenly from behind gigantic hanging leaves, like funhouse spooks.

We hauled our wares by sack and wagon, meandering through the countryside over the safe passes. There were quicker routes, but few dared to hasten their journey across lands they called *redfields* or *sinks*. Those lands belonged to the lissur. We wandered in drunk with fatigue, like soldiers from a Wilfred Owen poem, wearing clothes heavy with rain and painted black with soil that clung like tar to our pant legs.

We did this because it was our chance to be a community again. It was our one chance for something we hadn't been in so long. It was our chance to be normal.

A canopy of arboreal growth shielded us enough to conduct business even on the wettest days. Market was a time when all the richness of our new home was on display to be sampled and bartered for. Thousands of edible species of flora and many marvelously succulent combinations previously untouched by human tongues—the absinthian croakweed and the sweetgreens, the moist red crellets and the striped jala fruit that positively dripped with flavor—all set up in bushels. The strange and grotesque fauna lined the stalls. Horned and winged creatures hung from pikes while others buzzed and squawked from cages. Fat, hairy drootmunks and flying poppits lay encased in thick tree wine.

The hard-shelled and soft-bodied children of Eden, things without limbs, without faces. Their songs, once so strange, were now all too familiar. But no tastes were in higher demand than those of Earth. And only I, The Meatman, could create the illusion of mammalian flesh. The surface of this planet held none. That it would come up out of the ground was the real surprise.

After all the probes, all the scanning, all the yottobytes of data on Eden's surface, this spot was chosen for the colony. The plans were made. The ships launched. But we never anticipated what was twisting around in the deep dark just below us.

The lissur—dirt dragons—were a surprise, indeed. Hideous, awful, bloodthirsty creatures. We soon discovered dozens of different breeds, but, no matter which breed, their nature was the same. Mindless, soulless, bottomless wells of stinking death. They fired themselves up from the bowels of this hell to feed on the living. To feed on us. And now, without them, I was nothing in this new world.

Bean and I laid the meat out on the stones for barter.

"You never answered me before. Are you going to send me back to Father Hy?" he asked. "I'm not getting any better."

"You're always welcome to stay on, you know that. I told your father not to put his faith in the meat."

My perceived good health, over many years, gave rise to the popular belief that the less *native* something tasted, the less it would allow the disease to ravage our bodies. This was rubbish, of course. My body was hairy and I constantly wore a shadow of dirt, so my skin hadn't appeared to discolor like the others. In mine, the palest of blue eyes, the flecking that always manifested at the onset of the disease did not always show. I was outwardly a healthy, entirely human man. But make no mistake, Eden's sickness was inside me. I could feel it setting in.

My people didn't want to see that, though. They wanted to believe in The Meatman, the one who eats the beasts, the one who had escaped Eden's curse. It was a lie. A lie I never invented or promoted, but one I benefited from nonetheless. I didn't keep them free from the disease. I kept them free from hopelessness. It was the best I could do.

"There's nothing miraculous about this stuff, Bean. You know that now better than anyone. It's just flesh and ingredients. Never put your faith in it."

"Father always says his faith is with you…not that low serpent." The boy's voice deepened, mimicking Father Hy's baritone. "Work with The Meatman, my son, and your soul will remain always divine." He laughed and slapped another piece of meat down onto the table.

The boy's biological had become a spiritual figure in our community, but Father Hy, as he came to be known, hadn't always been a holy man. He came to Eden, like so many others in Alpha colony, to dig in the dirt. Like me, he only found his calling after a need arose. Eden had a way of doing that, turning us settlers into the people we were intended to be all along. As for myself and religion…well, I never had a strong need to be talked to in riddles.

"Your soul will remain always divine?" I said. "What exactly did he mean by that?"

"As long as my body and mind stay human, my

soul survives. That's what he thinks." Bean dropped another slab of meat but this one slid across the rock and found its way onto the ground. "I'm sorry."

"It's all right," I said.

"I can't even do the simple things anymore."

"It's fine, Bean." The boy was tired. Anyone could see that. "Why don't you catch a quick nap."

"Really? You don't mind? But market's set to open soon."

"I don't mind, go get you some rest," I said. "Besides, I can't have you dropping product all day. You'll be right as rain in an hour."

I let him sleep on my empty pack behind our table while I finished displaying the meat.

4

"Point out your choicest cuts," a burly farmer said, leering over my table in the blaring midday light. His eyes were hazed over in a chrome-colored film and he got his face down close to the meat to examine it. The span of his reach was so great he could pluck two pieces off either end of the table simultaneously. "These are some fine pieces you've got here, Meatman, just fine. We'll eat real good this month, wife."

They were long-time afflicteds. He was known as Reaper. She was Handy. They perused the scraps on the stone table while their brood of thirteen milled about behind them. They all stared at the meat with the same absent, quicksilver gaze. Their limbs were elongated and, though their clothes made an attempt to hide them, stubby protrusions had budded underneath. The chartreuse skin color that every diseased settler acquired had given way in this family to a tougher, umber coat marked by white striations. It was the final stage of the change. *Sugar and stripes*, they called it.

They were good people and as much as I pitied them, I'd be a liar if I said their presence didn't also disgust me. From the copious number of grimaces and catcalls, I wasn't alone.

"One cut is as good as another," I said first, then, more loudly to the passersby, "If it's not the finest cut, it doesn't make my table."

Reaper pointed out four pieces.

An anonymous male voice said, "All the steak on Eden won't fix that lot."

Reaper turned.

A group stood loosely huddled behind the family. At the front was a sturdy, handsome woman of some years. She wore spectacles and a sack of a dress with a high-rise collar, even in the heat season. Tradition demanded Cardinal Justices dress partly in red while out amongst the public, but the Lady Malic insisted on covering herself in the sanguine hue from hair to heel. The men surrounding her kept a few feet of open air between themselves and the lady at all times.

"You'd be wise, Mr. Reaper, to take your soulless eyes off me," she said without looking up from the knob of caprilla fruit in her hand. She twirled the ripened, speckled delicacy, inspecting it. "Considering your condition, I wouldn't expect you to be so *thin-skinned*." The men chuckled.

A justice was always blunt.

Handy tugged on her husband's sleeve and grumbled something I couldn't quite make out. Reaper stepped toward Lady Malic, but her entourage quickly filled the space between the two. Her men consisted of several, healthy, land-tough farmers, their hair long and streaked with sweat.

The Lady Malic calmly explained, "There's no quarrel here, Mr. Reaper, so please don't be foolish and create one. Pick out your meat and be on your way and I give you my word that you and your family won't be subjected to any more harassment here today. You must understand though how the sight of you people unnerves folks around here."

Reaper only stared back at the Cardinal Justice. A prodigiously tall bowman, almost as big as Reaper himself, stepped forward. He raised one bulging arm and reached behind his head to pluck an arrow from his quiver. "Lady Malic, allow me to remove—"

"My word was given, Chamberlain," the woman said with an icy deliberateness. "That's all you need hear."

The loyalty chip implanted in the bowman's head clicked on, and the archer dropped his arm, fed it between his bow and string then threw the apparatus over his shoulder. "Of course, m'lady. Sincerest apologies."

New settlements needed order. Chamberlain kept the colony in order for Lady Malic, and the chip kept Chamberlain in order.

The men fanned out behind Lady Malic again as Reaper's face twisted into an angry knot. Bean was watching from behind our table, enthralled by the conflict.

"Packs need to be cleaned or they'll reek of worm meat," I told him. "Why don't you take them down to the brook and wash them out now."

"Can't it wait a few minutes?"

"Take them now," I said.

Bean huffed once then stomped off, but the boy did exactly as he was told. He always did.

Onlookers began to gather as Lady Malic's words failed to quell the situation. She decided to address the growing crowd. "As your appointed Justice, my promises must be as solid as twistwood and my judgments as fair as the summer sky. Have I not been a trustworthy and just Cardinal?" Many murmurs of agreement came from the assemblage. "A Cardinal Justice has only her word with which to rule."

"Her word?" Reaper roared. "Yes, our poor Cardinal Justice has only her word... and a loaded streaker under her belt, to go along with that loyalty-chipped lapdog." Reaper pointed a thumb in the direction of the men. "And this bunch of halfwits."

Lady Malic turned back to the farmer. "More

complaints?" she asked.

Reaper moved closer. "We all came here together, and we're all going out the same way. This ain't the right manner to treat people." He pointed to the crowd. "And all of you know it!" Then he said quietly to his wife, "They don't have to buy my crops, but I'll be damned if I'm going to let them insult us."

"Goodness me, Reaper," Lady Malic said. "Stop whining before you make an old woman cry."

The people burst into laughter. Handy tugged her husband's arm again and shook her head. "The little ones are scared. Just let it be now, husband." She gathered the children up close to her.

Reaper stroked the deep brown gouges of his wife's cheek. "It's not fair," he said, exasperation in his voice. "Forgive me, wife, but what else can I do?"

Suddenly, he sprung at Lady Malic, his huge frame covering the distance between them in less than an instant. He clamped his fingers around her arms, squeezed them to her sides, and lifted the woman off the ground, spinning her away from the pack and planting her in front of my table. He bent down until the tips of their noses nearly met. "Eden's stronger than you, *m'lady*. And there's going to be more and more of us before this is over. That still means something." Reaper released the startled woman just as her men got a hold of him.

"No," she said. "Let him be."

Chamberlain's loyalty chip clicked on, and he immediately let Reaper go. The other men followed suit as the huge farmer tore his body away. Reaper gathered up his family to leave, and the men followed.

"No!" Lady Malic repeated. "My word was given. Let them go... for now." Chamberlain cordoned the men off with his outstretched arms as she bellowed to the family, "Best you keep your infection far from market!"

Many in the crowd bristled with an identical sentiment. "Go live in the bushwoods where you belong!" was a cry echoed by the group. "You're not one of us!"

The Reapers hurried off into the forest without looking back.

Lady Malic took a heavy breath and pulled a kerchief from her pocket to dab the sweat from her forehead. She called her men to my table then turned to face me. "I'm sorry," she said.

I waved my hand. "No need."

"No, I'm afraid there is a need, a great one. There are those among us who would be better suited keeping to themselves instead of exposing us all to the melancholy that is their lives."

"They've got a right to eat, don't they?" I asked.

Lady Malic threw me a sideways glance as she fingered some meat. "Normally I would tell you to leave the interpreting of rights to the experts, but I get your angle. A good customer is a good customer."

"That's right."

Lady Malic noticed Bean as he labored up the hill with the wet packs on his shoulders. She motioned to him. "And good help is hard to find," she said. "No matter what they look like."

"Right again," I said.

"Being a provider doesn't always allow for high-minded thinking, I suppose. If it did, there wouldn't be a need for Justices."

"Oh, I don't know, Cardinal, there's always got to be a job for someone who can do all the high-minded thinking for us."

My statement pulled a lifeless chuckle out of her.

"Do you ever wonder what it'll be like when there aren't any customers left?" She slapped a lump of meat onto the table. "That's a tasty one, don't you think?"

Of course I'd wondered about it, the end of our colony. Who hadn't? We were dying a lot faster than we were reproducing. You didn't have to be much of a mathematician to figure that equation.

"It's yours," I told her. "Let me wrap it." I laid the meat inside an oversized sunsplash leaf and tied the ends together neatly.

"I haven't offered barter yet."

"Just consider me paid up on my taxes," I said.

"Don't be silly, Meatman, I'm a public servant. You've already paid quite enough," she said before her countenance darkened. "Of course, in times of crisis our debt to the community can't solely be covered in goods. There are times when our *service* is required as well." She glanced at the macabre feast dripping crimson juice off the side of the rock. "Lovely looking things—you're profoundly skilled." She wiped the faux blood from the table with her finger then licked it clean. "Men of skill, that's precisely what we'll need in the coming days."

Now I wasn't accustomed to people looking me in the eye anymore, but Lady Malic seemed completely unfazed by my aura. Or was it just that she had a bigger one than me? This woman had irises like burned-out holes, and when she stared into mine it felt like she was crawling right down inside me to make certain I understood that the services she required from me would not be pleasant, no sir. You don't hire a hunter to polish your china. You call on a hunter because they're not afraid to get their hands bloody.

As I stared back into that expanse of piceous matter she called eyes, I swear I saw nothing I could relate to.

I wonder what was it that she saw inside me?

5

The day's trading had been brisk and as the sun hung low on a bruise-colored horizon, Bean and I packed up my newly bartered goods. I got a necklace for Nessa. It was little more than a heart-shaped lump of polished stone, but I knew it would bring a smile to her face. It also distracted my mind from Lady Malic's words. But it was a long slog home, with plenty of time to think. I pulled out my stub of pencil and jotted down some thoughts before we left:

I hated Eden. I hated watching it eat away at us. None of us had any illusions coming here; we knew we'd lead hardscrabble lives at first. But there had been hope for a happiness that had disappeared on Earth. There were to be more transports—every few months—bringing settlers and provisions. We would need new stocks of food, medicine, weapons—this much we'd known. But there were so many other things we'd need. Things we could only know of once we spread roots and lived in this world. And if Eden rejected us and all our careful planning and advanced technologies? If it just spit us back out into the void— what then? At the very least we'd need a ride home.

That was seventeen years ago.

No new transports ever arrived, not even word as to why. What happened? The answer might have meant something before our supplies ran out. After that, we were too busy figuring out ways to survive. We all became a little less human then. Long before Eden got into our blood.

It's hard to believe now but I respect Cardinal Malic. She was one of us. She made sacrifices. She took losses. She was smart, creative. She was an unmitigated bitch, and she survived. Nobody likes to admit it, but someone's got to be in charge. Everyone hates *the man*, even when it's a woman.

On Earth they fought over land, over water. They fought over money. They fought to see who had the biggest gun, who had the biggest god. We were chosen to be Alpha colony because we were all on the same side. Cardinal Malic was our leader. She was just what we needed to survive in a place like Second Eden.

Bean snapped me out of my reverie. "Did you hear those Digger boys over on Sanctuary Hill found a whole house buried in the ground?"

"How far underground?" I asked.

"Just a few feet. They think maybe it was a mudslide. They found pictures in there too, old drawings of the hillside. I saw them. The bush doesn't look the same in those pictures. It's taller now, and fuller. In the pictures it looks like it was just starting to grow. Those drawings didn't come from us. They came from whoever was here *before* us."

"Makes you wonder, doesn't it? Maybe we weren't the first to try to settle here after all. I got a feeling this place is just full of secrets."

"Well I want to know what happened to those people, where they went." His voice got low. "If that's where I'm going."

I put my hand on his shoulder. "I'd bet you cash money we all end up in the same place eventually."

"Where's that?"

"I don't know. Heaven, maybe, if you believe in a place like that."

"How do you know if you're in Heaven?"

I shook my head and laughed. "So, so many questions, my young Bean."

"I'm serious. I want to know. How will I be able to tell if I'm in Heaven?"

I let out a loud sigh and thought a moment. "All right," I said. "Close your eyes." The boy obliged. He always did. "Shut everything else out except the sound of my voice."

"Okay," he said.

"Now turn your ears inside out and listen very closely. Listen to the voices *inside* you, speaking to you. I know someone who hears the voices and it eases her mind to listen to them. You hear them too, don't you?"

"How do you know about the voices?" he asked.

"Never mind," I told him. "Just listen to them. Ask *them* your question."

If Eden's voices weren't lies, like Nessa believes, then   this was the one time when they might actually do our kind some good. Bean shut his eyes tight and didn't speak at all for a minute or two.

"What are you seeing?"

"They're showing me a place," he said, "with a lot of people. Is this Heaven?"

"Do you know the people?"

"Yes, some of them."

"Do you care about all these people?"

The boy grinned. "Yes."

"Then it's Heaven," I said. "It might go by a different name to other folks, but if you're there with all the people you ever cared about, then you're definitely in Heaven."

Bean opened his eyes and smirked at me. "I know what you're trying to do and I appreciate it, but I'd still like to know where all the people really disappear to."

I nodded at him. "Me, too. You know there was a legend back home about old elephants who would walk to a place they'd never been to before—

sometimes hundreds of miles away—just to lie down and die. Maybe that's the way it is here too."

"What's an elephant?" Bean asked.

I smiled. "It doesn't really matter."

"Oh, okay then," he said. "Then could you tell me what *cash money* is?"

My god, I never realized how old thirty-eight could feel.

6

The storms here are gentle, mostly. Not like on Earth, where a cold New England sleet would stiffen you up and have you running for shelter. Here, warm pellets gently shower you. The sound of them bouncing off the land is a sheet of white noise, drowning out everything else. The entire experience is immersive, womblike, and hypnotic. It lulls you into feeling you're safe out there in the open. Eden needs you that way so it can have its children tear you to pieces. That's how it feeds.

Bean and I were out of the lush bushwoods and the forest no longer insulated our movements. Our naked footfalls fell on sodden ground—a distinctive pattern, permeating the soil to its bowels, as different from the rain patter as black is from white. The miry ground only served to slow the boy more.

I skirted my gaze along the horizon for any signs of danger. "Let's pick it up."

The lissur were unthinking beasts, but what they lacked in intelligence they made up for in brutal instinct and honed adaptation. Nature constructed these creatures to reign here. It wouldn't take them long to find us. I was armed up to my eyes, as usual. But steel wasn't everything.

"Do you want me to carry you?"

"No, sir," Bean said. The boy marshaled his strength, grunting loudly with each step.

Through the dim shreds of light piercing the clouds, I caught the glint of starstone veining through a cluster of grassy buttes that humped the horizon. It was far away, maybe too far for Bean. In the redfields, the only haven from the lissur was Edenrock, as it protected us from direct subterranean attacks and the flat tops made for excellent footing. But these were the redfields, and there wasn't much rock to be found in them. We were at least a little bit lucky to find something. Still, at the familiar vibrato that hummed through the ground and up my legs, my heart surged with dread.

A lissur was here.

I turned my legs into pistons, and my feet disappeared into the ground with each step I pumped into that bog. Bean was falling farther behind. I looked back to find the boy's twig legs clopping desperately on my oversized siltshoes. Even through the platinum coat of pulp that covered his eyes, I saw the presence of fear. He was still all-too-human. Too human to die like this. I wouldn't allow it. So I doubled back to fetch him.

The low rumble was all around us now. The serpent was nipping at our toes. I reached Bean, snatched his hand, and tugged, but the boy was like an anchor.

"Try to move," I demanded.

"No," he said. He pulled his hand loose from mine and his arms fell limp. His face was awash in an eerie serenity.

And the thumping grew.

"Go. You don't have much time," he said. "My father wants me to die human, with a soul. That's all he cares about. Why do you think he sent me to you? He never put his faith in the meat to cure me. He put his faith in you to let me die before I changed."

"Then your father's going to be awfully disappointed with me," I said. I swiped at his arm, but he pulled it back again. So I charged him, buried my shoulder into his midsection, and wrapped my arms around his waist. With every drop of life I had left inside me, I lifted his body and tossed him over my shoulder, draping him around the back of my neck like a scarf.

But as I took a quick step my leg sunk into the soil below my knee. I needed my siltshoes back. When I dropped Bean and madly tried to unlace the shoes from his feet, the mud began to tremble. I knew I couldn't have them off before the lissur surfaced.

"On your feet!" I told him. "You have to run for it." I pointed to the butte. "If we can get close enough to those—"

The ground bulged, lifting Bean into the air, then cracked and fell away in chunks beneath his feet, leaving a man-sized hole. A baleful smell, rancid and wild, rose from the fractured terra. With a series of violent jerks, Bean's lower body disappeared into the pit.

"No!"

My heart adrenalized and beat more furiously, threatening to explode from my chest. There were no other options now. I reached inside my shirt and unsheathed the saber from its scabbard. I'd never wished to strike a truer blow.

I raised the saber to the sky. I took aim. I swung.

The blade easily broke through the hardened body shingles that encased Bean. It cleaved the soft of his neck flesh and severed his bony chord. Finally, it burst out the other side amidst a spray of splintered skin. No sooner had his head been freed than the boy's body sagged and slid, arms raised, beneath the mud. His dead fingers towed the head until it, too, was swallowed up in the Eden-soil.

It was a well-struck blow. For that I was thankful. That alone.

Then I ran. To have done anything else would have been folly. Without Bean to slow me, I had a chance. It was a foul and uncaring thought, but it was true. So I sheathed my saber and made for the safety of the starstone and surer footing.

This lissur was quick. Probably small. As it burrowed closer to the surface, and to me, the land mounded behind the streaking animal. The dark ground juddered to such an extreme that I was no longer held in its grip with each step, but rather, my feet became *unstuck* due to the reverberations. It sped me considerably, and I splashed across the field.

The land thickened, and soon my shoes were slapping against solid stone. I vaulted across its glittering surface, reached a small rock face, and scrambled to the outcropping's top before rolling onto my back, swallowing the warm, heavy air.

Couldn't stop yet. I had to get up.

I flipped over and got to my feet. Reaching inside my coat, I tapped my arsenal of weaponry with my fingers, choosing a blade for each hand. I drew a rapier for my left and a small scythe for my right. Atop the butte the tremors were faint, but the lissur's vibrating song was still present.

Then it stopped.

From my perch, I scanned the landscape, snuffing the air like a hound. I spun around just as a russet-colored torpedo head emerged from the gravel, propelled from below by a collection of short, floppy legs. A King Quintha lissur. Big nasties, these were. This one was still young though, as evidenced by its circumference and mottled skin. It emerged from the hole, lifting itself by its legs, to rise several feet above my head and study me with a ring of a hundred, large, white eyes peaking out from behind upturned scales. Their eyes were always pure white—like huge, embedded eggs. Shaking furiously, the lissur gave a prolonged hiss.

There's no lack of edge to you, is there, you little bastard?

An outer layer of skin at its tip peeled back to expose a great maw. The ruddy, folded flesh within it a stark contrast to its darkly-mirrored exterior. From inside the tip, toothy tendrils unfurled, engorged with poison, and the whole putrid mass swung closer. On hardened ground and with my weapons already drawn, I was more prepared than I could've hoped to be. If I was to fall, this lissur would have earned it.

With my rapier, I delivered a controlled thrust into an endocrine pouch deep within the beast's mouth and the hormone that holds much of the creature's bile leaked out. Now pacified, I swayed my hands rhythmically in front of the tendrils, the way a snake charmer might, allowing them to entwine the blades. Adjusting the swords slowly to and fro at practiced angles, I coaxed the tendrils down onto the starstone.

Sleep, little one. Go to sleep.

Then I slid my rapier out and laid it across the top of the writhing nest to hold the tendrils in place. Slowly, I raised the scythe, then dropped it hard, severing each veiny stalk and leaving the remains to retreat into the Quintha's angry mouth.

As the tendrils flailed about like stray hoses, they spat their lifeblood at me. I hacked at the lissur with the scythe until all the fight had left the young King. When it tried to descend back under the rock, I dropped both rapier and scythe and pulled two serrated daggers with balloon hilts from my belt. I drove them into either side of the animal. As the lissur burrowed, the daggers caught at the surface and the hilts kept it from submerging. With it partially topside and struggling, I jumped from my perch and reached for Fin, the parashu axe I kept strapped between my shoulder blades. I fingered its haft before lifting the axe out and burying the curved bit into the lissur.

I yanked the blade free and swung again, and again, and again. I chopped away until the remaining topside portion of the serpent fell, spraying mud and juice across my legs. Then I staked the meat to the ground and completed the detachment with my knife. The remaining diaphanous stump slid down the hole and disappeared meekly into the darkness.

It was over.

I kicked the lifeless meat, stabbed it, hammered and screamed at it. I owed the boy that much. I owed the boy my anger. I owed it to myself, too. I stayed there alone, sitting on my knees in the mud for a long while.

It was over. Bean was gone.

I lifted the meat onto my shoulder and headed back.

7

It was late when I returned home. Nessa was still bound to the bed. I clumsily plucked at her ligatures while she glowered.

"Is Bean in the shed?"

"The kid couldn't hack it anymore, so I sent him home." I swallowed hard. "He won't be coming back."

"That's a real shame," she said. "It must've been hard for you to let him go. I know how much you liked him."

I turned away and rubbed at my eyes. "I didn't have much choice."

She waited while I freed her arms then said, "Jon, I don't want to be tied down anymore."

I stamped my foot. "You don't know what you're saying. Listen, I'm sorry I'm late. The market was heavy today," I said. "I brought you something though." I pulled the necklace from my pocket and handed it to her.

She gripped it in her fist then threw it across the bedroom. "I don't want these straps on me anymore."

"Is it the nightmares again?" I unclasped the final harness that fettered her ankle.

"They're not nightmares, they're visions. Visions of something to come for me. I'm not scared of it anymore. I'm not scared of anything... except being tied up alone here." Her body fell at my feet. "Please, don't you want me to find some peace before I leave?"

"You're not going anywhere," I said. "I won't let you." I thumped my fist repeatedly against the wall behind me. "I won't let you go. I won't do it!"

The room fell silent because in our hearts I think we both knew that what I wanted wasn't the way things worked out on Eden. The disease would take her eventually, whether I tied her down or not. I picked her back up onto the bed and lay beside her when she took my head and cradled it to her breast.

"I should have given you children," she said. "They would have been beautiful."

I nodded softly and sat up. Nessa's arms were still wrapped around me. "It may be better you didn't." I told her. "This place is turning everyone into madmen. Malic brought her crew to market today, stirring things up. These people--*our friends*--are getting ugly, Nessa."

"I don't like leaving you this way," she said.

I don't know what happened then. Was it her words? Or was it something in her voice, that ravaged voice, that caused me to snap? I clenched my teeth. "I'm not letting you leave. The bush can call out to you all it wants, but you're staying with me. Maybe it'll slow down, or stop."

She untangling herself from me and stood up. She slid out of her nightgown naked and stretched her arms out to her sides. Frosted streaks covered her. Her thickened midsection, riddled with uneven knobs that stuck way out like the sides of a coat rack, robbed her of all the femininity she once had. The sickness spread all the way to her feet, where her toes were now gnarled and overgrown, entwined with one another, reaching out in all directions.

I closed my eyes.

"This is me. This is what I am now," she said. "How can you still fight this? I've stopped. You should, too."

I touched her fingers gently, kissed the thick, tawny skin inside her wrist, and pulled her back onto the bed beside me. "If I give you up, what's left?" I eased her hand above her head and, before she could protest, buckled it into the strap.

"Don't do this. I belong to them," she said. My stomach turned. "I'm not yours to fight for anymore, I'm already Eden's slave. Don't make me yours, too."

A knock came loudly at the door.

My heart leapt. "Stay in bed. If the wrong person sees you like this...just stay here." I sprung from the room then grabbed a machete from its mount on the wall before throwing open the door.

Lady Malic stood hooded and dripping at the threshold with much of her gang gathered several feet behind her. "Gracious," she said, catching sight of my knife, "looks like you've got yourself in a stew." She flashed a thin-lipped grin. "Must be your wife— only a woman could get a man so bent. No matter, you hold on to that fire, it'll be of good use tonight. I'm taking the boys over to Reaper's farm." She turned away. "Exquisite almond blossom tree you have out here, Meatman. Eden-soil clearly agrees with it."

I lowered the machete. "It shot up like a rocket as soon as I put her in the ground," I told her. "Reaper's farm, eh? That's a hell of a walk in this stuff. You're probably better off just staying put." If I could get this group back in their beds tonight, tomorrow might have them looking at this situation with leveler heads.

Lady Malic sighed and stepped back into the rain. Chamberlain then slipped by her and leaned in through the doorframe, his ever-present bow and quiver clinging to his back. "Your service as a guide is being requested by the office of the Cardinal Justice."

"Only requested?" I asked.

Chamberlain stared at me. "*Required.* Now if you please..." he stepped out of the doorway and extended his arm into the open air for me to follow.

I glanced toward the bedroom, praying Nessa hadn't been seen. "Just let me tell my wife." I swung the heavy door but Chamberlain wedged his siltshoe in before it could close.

"Would you mind terribly if we waited inside?" Lady Malic asked. "This rain wears on me."

Nessa blared at us in that wretched garble of hers, "Give me a moment." A clatter escaped the bedroom.

I called out, "It's the Cardinal Justice and those friends of hers I told you about earlier." The noise quickly stopped. *Smart girl.* "I have to go with them," I shouted again to her. "They need a guide."

A long silence, and then her answer, "Hurry back."

"She sounds awfully raw," Lady Malic said, wiping her glasses clean. "We have Doc Cutter with us." She waved the man forward. "Why don't you let him take a look at her."

"If you think she sounds raw now, wait until you come in here with those siltshoes on—she'll have me scrubbing these floors the minute I get back. No, we should just get going. She's got a hoarse cold is all. Give me a minute to load up and say goodbye, and I'll get us on the trail."

Malic smiled and gave the signal. "Suit yourself."

Chamberlain edged his foot out from between the door and its frame. I closed it carefully then rushed to the bedroom.

"Are they gone?" Nessa asked.

"Not without me." I grabbed her arms and stretched them over the headrest to where the bindings attached to the wall. Then I closed the straps around her wrists.

"What are you doing? Don't do this again. This isn't what you really want for us, is it, Jon?"

"Maybe not," I said. "But it's what I've got." I finished the task at her ankles, and she flopped and arched her body like a fish caught on a dock. "I'm sorry. This is the only way. I need to get these people as far away from you as I can." I kissed her lips and her imprisoned body dropped to the bed in defeat.

From off the wall, I snatched every bit of weaponry I could carry and affixed them to my hunting vest. Then I stuffed my journal inside my coat pocket and left with Lady Malic and the men—nine in all—to begin the slow journey to Reaper's spread. The rain had been on a steady pour all night, turning the land into a slough. My body was wearing down, but there was no time to rest.

8

We'd been humping it for more than an hour when Lady Malic shouted through the din of falling raindrops, "Meatman, are you certain this is the most direct route?"

"*Most* direct?" I yelled back. "No, but it's the safest."

One of the men, Owen All, threw his hands up. "I must be going deaf. Did you say we *weren't* on the quickest path? Why the hell not?"

"Because we wouldn't make it," I barked at him. "Well, *you* wouldn't make it."

Owen looked at the Cardinal like a dog who'd just had his nose slapped. Lady Malic told him, "If the Meatman says you wouldn't make it, then I believe you would not make it, Owen."

"You're welcome to try," I said, pointing in a southeasterly direction.

Owen grumbled and fell back with the others, leaving me with Lady Malic and Chamberlain at the front of the pack. She cackled loudly. "You don't suffer fools gladly, Meatman. I knew there was something about you I liked."

"I suppose I don't," I said. "Can I ask how you're holding up so far?"

"Oh, I'm hardier than I might appear. You needn't worry about me."

"I'm not worried. I'm just asking."

"It's appreciated," the woman said, and we continued to walk. "You know, an army needs generals, and generals need their soldiers." She motioned with her head to the men. "But generals also need lieutenants."

I raised an eyebrow. "After all these years I've kind of gotten used to being a free-thinking man, ma'am. I'm my own general, lieutenant, sergeant, colonel, and corporal all in one. It suits me." I tapped a finger against the side of my head. "You won't find any loyalty chips in here, so I'm afraid I'm not wired the right way to be in your army. Besides, I thought Chamberlain here was your right-hand man."

The archer gave me a cold look.

"He is my right hand, and a damn fine one at that. I think he'd be the best man for the job even without that chip in his head," she said. "But I've got *two* hands."

"You make it sound like we're at war."

Her face soured. "Don't play coy, Meatman. We've been at war with this planet ever since we touched down, you know that. And Eden needs to secure soldiers for its army, too. The Reapers have one foot in the bush as it is. If we're going to beat this place, we don't need them, or anyone else, fighting for the other side."

I stopped walking. My voice was eager, like a child's, when I asked her, "What are you saying exactly—that you think the Alphas are still alive after the bush takes them? How do you know this?"

"Alive? Yes, I think so, but not human. Once they disappear they'll be Eden's. And they'll protect their own. It's time we did the same." Placing her hand on my elbow, she started me walking again. "If you believe the stories—"

"People tell lots of stories about what's in the bush. Doesn't mean any of it's true. No one's spent more time in the bush than me and I haven't seen anything of our people."

"Well then maybe it's that you haven't suffered enough yet," she said, her voice eerily quiet. "I've felt things—mossy things creeping in the night, eyes watching from the wood. I tell you we're not alone, and whatever *they* are, they're getting stronger with every soul we give them. They'll come for the rest of us, the healthy ones, soon enough, you watch."

I shook my head. "I didn't take you for the superstitious sort, Cardinal."

"I believe in what I see," she said before halting abruptly. Lady Malic stopped the cortege then signaled to Chamberlain.

The marksman took a small glowing pouch from his longcoat and tied it to the shaft of one of his arrows. Pulling back his bowstring, he took aim at a high middy tree. The arrow disappeared from his hand and sailed into the darkness of the bushwoods. Several seconds passed before the top of the middy exploded in a sea of phosphorescent green light.

"Why are we marking our path?" I asked him. "I could navigate these fields for you blindfolded."

"And if you don't make it back from Reaper's, who navigates then?" Chamberlain asked.

I turned to Lady Malic. "Why wouldn't I make it back?"

She gave Chamberlain a severe look. "Your job is to listen and act, not talk." She shooed him away.

"What are you planning to do when we get to Reaper's farm?" I asked.

"Only what needs doing."

The idea, grotesque as it was, seemed less so now that the sick were considered a threat. I shook my head.

"I don't care what words passed between you and Reaper at market, he's still a man, and those are still his wife and children. You can't just get rid of them

"I'm sparing them," she said. "Before it's too late."

"But those were your people once. The people you swore to protect."

"That is precisely what I'm doing, my boy, protecting them from Eden's unholy plague. You don't make it to many of Father Hy's sermons, do you?"

"I don't get to church much," I said. "In these sermons, does he happen to mention who's going to save the rest of us when there's hardly anyone left in the colony?"

A smile broke across the Lady Malic's face. She must have been terrible at poker. "Haven't you wondered why we're the least affected?" she asked.

I was too embarrassed to tell her that just so long as people thought it was the meat that kept them more human, the real reason never occurred to me.

She went on, "My theory is that something in our genes wards off the disease. I'm convinced of it. Cutter and I are of a like mind on this."

"You say *theory* when *guess* is what you really mean. Where's the proof?"

She shrugged. "None of us are experts, but I feel like the connection is right there." She gave me a sideways glance. "I realize you've made a name for yourself fostering just the opposite belief."

"I never claimed my meat was a cure, if that's what you're getting at."

"Hold on now, I'm not saying you did. I'm merely pointing out that there are plenty of folks who believe in what you do. You've got this backward. I'm paying you a compliment."

I took a few deep breaths. "Okay, let's say this theory you got is right. What do we do about it?"

"Well, if we can stay alive and breeding long enough, patterns should develop. With each generation, we'll get closer to figuring it out. But it'll take generations. We need to start with the healthiest among us."

"And the sick?"

"They're our greatest threat," she said. "And our greatest responsibility. We can't just hand them over to fight for the enemy. And don't they deserve to die with dignity, as human beings?"

I thought about Bean's final moments. Had I preserved his dignity when I cut him in two?

"I don't know that I can live with that, ma'am."

"Of course you can. That's all I want you to do, is live with it. Live and thrive like those almond blossom trees of yours," she said, grabbing my shoulder. "Pass down whatever's inside you keeping you healthy, spread your Eden-resistant seed, to your sons and daughters, so we can survive here and make it our home. You may have to take on multiple wives to do it, Meatman. All the immune will." She shook a clump of mud from the wiring of her siltshoe. "No one thinks of Mother Nature as a butcher when she kills off the weakest of the species—it's Darwinism, survival of the fittest. It's the natural order of things." As we walked on, she wrapped her arm around mine. "You've got Hy's boy helping you, and I know you're close to him. I'm not pretending this is going to be easy—it shouldn't be—but Eden hasn't given us any choice. This planet is raping itself into us, making us hard people. It's time to use that hardness to our advantage."

Lady Malic waited for me to speak, but there was nothing I could say, nothing I could force between my lips. I could only stare beyond her.

"Something holds you back," she said. "In time you'll see this is the way." She slipped her arm out from under mine then slowed her pace to fall back in with the rest of the group. "Lead on, Meatman," she told me with triumph in her voice.

What Lady Malic was selling made so much sense, it scared me. Even if I didn't agree with her completely, here was someone who finally had a plan. What if, in the future, we could rid our colony of the disease completely? Eventually create generations who are immune to it? What if we could beat this place--have something approaching normal lives? Hope is a dye; just a few drops in some water and you can color a whole well any shade you want. Still, the thought of being without Nessa in this new world crippled my hope. I couldn't imagine a life without her, much less a life where I'd allow someone to take her from me, even for the greater good. And yet with each step I took with this old woman and her family of followers, I felt a little less alone.

But after I cast my selfishness and fear aside and ignored all the philosophical claptrap, there was only the truth. When the good intentions were stripped from the bone, what we had at the Reapers would be a family slaughtered at our hands. And I couldn't change that. As I looked back at those men—their faces so full of fight, if only for the satisfaction of having put one up—I wondered if it occurred that way to any of them as well. I hope it did.

9

We were another hour in the mud before I spoke again. My skin was a wet sheet slung over muscle and my feet fell onto ground that was as soft as batter. Stopping briefly, I surveyed the land. "This gives way to black rock soon. It'll be easier to walk then. Reaper's place is just beyond that."

"Not to sound droll but, *well done*, Meatman." Lady Malic laughed to herself and lifted her siltshoes with a renewed spring.

Soft soil morphed into the ebon shine of volcanic stone and we sped to a trot before entering the scrublands behind the farm. The home was similar to many settlers' farmhouses, a small conglomeration of various Edenwood and brickstones, ramshackle with hasty repairs pocking the exterior like sores, tumoral additions bulging from its sides. The bush had invaded; vines slithered over the walls and crept into every aperture, growing and expanding, pressuring the brick, slowly ripping the home asunder from its core. Prismatic florets and a muscular sheath of cirri only served to disguise the fact that Eden's assault was ongoing here.

The sheets of warm rain mixed with a sea of steam and fog to mask any hint of our arrival. Lady Malic pointed out the side door of the farmhouse where a seepage of light crawled out from underneath into the pitch of night. She gave the signal and we gathered in front of it, steeling ourselves in preparation. Owen's lips stretched into a wicked smile, which spread to Lyin Cubb, his teenaged boy. Baxter, Guy Idler, The Frey, Smith, and Ackerman all gripped their cudgels tightly.

I had an uneasy feeling in my gut, like it was trying to tell me something. Something I wasn't allowing myself to hear. Lady Malic nodded to Chamberlain. The archer lifted a bent leg, cocked his knee back, and kicked open the door. We rushed through the house like water.

Reaper was the first. His appearance had altered even from that morning; he was larger and less human-looking, his frame filling the room. His midsection had widened, and his hands branched out into immense brown mitts. There were several jagged new arms now reaching from his trunk. When he saw us, his mangled vocal chords emitted a screech so shrill it startled us long enough for him to escape to the front room of the house.

Awestruck as we were, we gave chase.

He barricaded the narrow hallway with his body, flaring his extremities to the walls and ceiling. More screams—staccato, full of fear.

The group stopped dead twenty feet from him until, empty-handed, I approached the thing with my arms raised. His facial features had sunk into his skull and the lengthy protrusions that budded from his torso curled and flexed like dark, skinny fingers.

I said gently, "Let me talk to you."

"What are you doing? Owen said. "We didn't come here to talk to it."

I ignored his words and kept my focus on Reaper. "Maybe we can avoid all this," I said to the hulking mass.

The easement had barely passed my lips when his bony hands grabbed me. A number of his jagged arms reached down the hall and held me while the remainder wrapped themselves around my neck. I clutched at the wooden fingers puncturing my skin but couldn't pry them loose. As I struggled for air, the room began to go dark. I had to act. Breathing would have to wait a few more seconds.

With one hand, I freed my scimitar then wheeled it around my head, audibly slicing the thick air. I brought it through and severed the arm. Feeling the fingers immediately go limp, I tore them from my throat. I charged down the hall, leaped forward, and planted the sword into Reaper's left shoulder, a blow so well-struck it would have felled even the stoutest of men.

But this was no man, not anymore.

The blade lodged into his pulpy flesh and remained there. An amber syrup of lifeblood flowed from the wound. Frantically, I tried to remove the sword, but it was tightly embedded.

Although I feared his vengeance, Reaper took none. His face was strangely placid, his eyes empty. The men swarmed the hallway like ants, but Reaper was far heavier than he appeared and continued to block our passage. Smith tried to kick out his legs, but they seemed bonded to the floorboards, and we piled up in front of him.

"You're bottlenecked," Lady Malic shouted from outside the hall. "Somebody go round and cover the front door."

As more of Reaper oozed onto me, I loosed the scimitar from his body, yanking it upward, but he brought his hand down onto the blade and held it with a supernatural strength. His diseased face was straining and he growled at us. He was fighting for his family. And even if it wasn't completely human, it was admirable.

Our assault must have taken its toll on the giant though. A gap opened under one of Reaper's arms and Cubb squeezed past. Then Baxter slid through…then the rest of them.

Handy appeared in the hallway in front of us, a poker wrapped in her fist. She hadn't changed to the degree her husband had; she looked much the same as she did that morning, more than enough human to give a few of the men pause. As she shuffled forward, Ackerman wasted no time bludgeoning the woman before tipping her stiffened frame against the wall. She crashed against the wood with a dull *thud* then slid down.

Reaper turned his head toward me. The sight of his wife's corpse seemed to take any remaining fight out of him, and as I finally extracted my blade, he fell to the floor as well, the air escaping from his body in a hideous burble. Lying beside his wife, he looked directly at me and whispered a single word.

"*Never.*"

The wet wind howled through the front door, announcing the children's escape. When we got there, Chamberlain was pointing across the sward to the deep brush. "They were already out of the house when I came around," he said. "I didn't have time to bring any of them down, but they ducked in there."

One by one, we charged into the bushwoods hedging the front of the house. We hacked away at thick cables of vine and branches that crisscrossed our path like cage bars, often catching a glimpse of *something*. It was always just ahead of us though, darting through the soft moonbelt light that trickled through the bush. These glimpses carried us forward desperately through the nettles and brambles that tore away at each of us by inches.

"It hurts!" Cubb screamed, his disembodied voice floating among the trees.

My vision grew blurry and a hot pain ran through me as I staggered over the path of trampled vegetation and out of the bushwoods. Owen pulled his boy into the dark light of the clearing, and we huddled around him. Boils pushed out of his exposed skin. Someone else called from deep inside the briar. Lady Malic stood in the yard, waiting for the rest to emerge while Cubb lay on his back with his chest heaving.

"Help him, Cardinal. Somebody, please, help my boy," Owen said.

"Cutter, we need you out here now," she yelled. Then she paced around the men. "I can't believe we let those damned kids lead us right into a poison patch."

My arms swelled and searing lesions formed on my skin.

A voice cried out from the bush again, "I can't breathe."

Lady Malic paced between us. "Where the hell's Cutter?"

"I think that *is* Cutter, ma'am," Chamberlain told her, nodding to the bush. "Shall I fetch him?"

She waved the archer into the patch.

Ass down in the mud and waiting out the plant toxins, I took out my journal to write while Lady Malic corralled her troops, their faces filled to bursting with rosy pustules.

"Are we done?" she screamed. "Is this all it takes to stop you *men*—a few pricks and rashes?"

"No, Cardinal Justice," they said in near unison, their faces wet with rain.

Chamberlain emerged, covered in burrs, Cutter slung across his back, huffing desperately. Malic took a seat on the soil and instructed Chamberlain to lay the doctor on the ground in front of her, where she watched as his face twisted into a death rictus.

Lady Malic took a long moment before letting out a small groan as she lifted herself from her knees and then asked, "Is anyone else here going to die?"

No one answered.

"Is anyone else going to die on me?" she said again.

"No," a few voices answered her, and none of us did die. At least not in that field.

"What about the Reaper kids?" Guy Idler spit the words out through inflated lips.

"They're lost to us," Lady Malic said. "But tomorrow we'll go through the whole damned colony. We'll recruit the healthy and put down the rest!" She put her finger down onto my open journal. "Alpha colony's salvation started this night--write that down in your book."

I imagined Nessa in bed the next morning with a fanatical throng cresting the hill beside our house. I closed the journal and forced myself up. "I'm leaving."

"What?" Lady Malic said, "I still need you."

"No, you don't. If this crusade of yours fails just because I'm not there, then it was meant to die."

"The strong will survive this, Meatman, and strength will beget strength. Once the weak perish, they'll rid us of their rot. Have faith in that."

I cleared my throat. "Look maybe you're right, and maybe you're just stabbing at the truth. I really don't know. But you're talking about killing people I came here with—people you came with. We're all trying to stay more human, right? Then explain to me why I feel like less of a man now?"

Malic had no answer for me.

"Now, I'm not saying you're wrong, Cardinal—I'm not saying that at all. I'm just saying it's late, I miss my wife, and I'm just plain tired of listening to you talk.

It's time I got back home. Follow me or stay here, it makes no difference to me."

Lady Malic pursed her lips and waited a moment. "Gentlemen, what we have here is a case of receding spine. He might not be so closed off to our cause if he wasn't protecting his own."

My whole body started to shudder, but I hid it from them. It felt as if Malic's own icy fingers had grabbed hold of that receding spine she accused me of having.

"A blind woman could see that your Nessa's taken ill," she said.

Inside, my body was raging. My heart fluttered in my chest and dropped.

She knows.

There was silence. Then Malic waved her finger nonchalantly in my direction.

"Well, go get him before he decides to run off."

The men flanked me.

"Don't any of you touch my Nessa!" I gritted my teeth and pulled a blade with each hand, spitting and flailing.

A flying club caught the side of my head and brought me down. They were on me in an instant.

"Take his steel and keep him close," she told them. "Tonight's little hunting party has left me unfulfilled. I say why put off until tomorrow what can be started tonight. Let's pay a visit to your beloved Nessa."

The toxin-pain wore off and was replaced by a soreness my body had never known. With pikes at my ribcage, they led me back over the same route we'd just taken to Reaper's farm.

"What are you doing?" I said.

Lady Malic told her men, "If he speaks again, cut

out his tongue." Then she faced me. "I'm not saying you're wrong to ask, Meatman . . . I'm just tired of listening to you talk."

10

I knew what they were doing. I also knew this land in every direction for miles, so when we passed the last middy tree Chamberlain had marked and there wasn't a trace of phosphorescence to be found, I started to wonder.

Where were the markers?

It didn't really matter. If the trail was truly lost to them, they'd never find my house. It was just a matter of how long it would take *for them* to figure it out.

A little less than an hour of incompetent tracking later and Chamberlain had managed the task of throwing even me off my bearings. For the first time in years, I didn't recognize the land.

"How much longer to the first marker?" Lady Malic asked.

"We should've reached it by now, ma'am."

"Then why haven't we? Do you know where we are?"

Chamberlain didn't answer.

"Mr. Chamberlain, are we lost?"

"I believe we are," he finally said.

Lady Malic marched back to me and waved the men to lower their pikes. I was rubbing the soreness from my legs, anticipating that she was about to ask me where we were. Now it sounds like an easy thing to think up a lie on the spot, but when you're not practiced at such things, it turns out to be a lot harder than you'd expect. My mind was searching for a plausible mistruth when Malic began to speak, but before she could utter a word, a vibrato reached up through the mud and rattled our feet until our knees buckled.

"We need to get on solid ground," Chamberlain said with a flutter in his voice. He scanned in every direction. "Over there!"

The archer had spotted a ridgeline in the distance that was shrouded in shadow from those of us without the artificially-enhanced night eyes of his strigiforme vision. We raced for it, kicking up sludge just as the ground began to hum over the sound of the rain. Chamberlain scooped up the Lady Malic and dropped her over his shoulder. I didn't see any of the others. While I kept focused on the growing silhouette ahead, I'd passed the group, and I figured to be hitting a platform of ground rock soon. The ridgeline was just ahead.

Angry soil roared behind me and I craned my neck to watch a fissure open violently across the land and a spray of black liquid erupt like an oil strike, blotting out the light from the moonbelt. The glistening scales of several lissur broke the surface. They gulped the air then disappeared again. My heart pounding, the breath ripping from my lungs, I kept making for the bluffs just ahead, waiting for the rock to materialize beneath my feet. The lissur were close. Too close.

Fear and adrenaline fueled me. My mind was bewildered. My body—tempered muscle and sinew, the only things I could trust—controlled my movements. The bluffs were less than a hundred feet away now. Even without ground rock to save me, I could climb to the top of the ridge and hold out until morning, or until the monsters left.

The world shook with a deafening fierceness. My nerve endings had all been numbed by the sound. I peeked behind me again. The men lurched forward, wild-eyed, punching through raindrops, reaching for the stony oasis somewhere ahead of them. The marshy land finally began to harden. I tried to gain my footing, but my ankles folded over and my knees waggled.

I fell hard.

This ground wasn't smooth like blackrock. It was corrugated with roots. And they were moving.

I looked up with unbelieving eyes as the rock formation directly in front of me transmogrified and stood. Dozens of slender figures slowly unfolded themselves and splintered off from the whole. The low creak of great weight accompanied each of their movements. They stretched out their immense limbs and unfurled hidden foliage. Somewhere in that stirring, dark collection of leaves I could almost make out the faces that we'd lost. As those pitiless visages looked at the group, they pulled their rooted legs from the sod and gave slow, lumbering chase.

We fled from these new behemoths of Eden, the enemy Lady Malic had warned us about. But the trees marched toward us with the deliberateness of time and, like that very passage of time, we could not escape them. Every step they took covered a field. It was clear there was no sanctuary left, so we circled the leg of one and tried to climb its trunk; but it reached down and, with the swipe of one leaf-encrusted arm, removed us utterly.

The beings attacked. Their legs clopped slowly in the mush and their roots dragged behind them like loose shoelaces. We tried to scatter, but serpentine vines wrapped themselves around us and pinned our feet to the ground. And the air echoed with the sound of dragonsong.

Lady Malic, that tough old crow, wriggled an arm loose and picked up a machete. But instead of hacking herself out of her bonds, she tossed the weapon at *my* feet. "Get the Meatman his steel," she cried.

The men did exactly as they were told, and a pile quickly grew before me, hopping in time with the lissurs's subterranean movements directly below us. I grabbed a blade and slashed at the viny shackles until I was free.

"Cut us out. We'll help you," Ackerman said.

Although it pained me to acknowledge it, this bloodthirsty group was my people, and I needed them now. So I chopped away the ivy and gathered the group into a tight circle.

"Listen to me. Stay in formation. We fight back-to-back. Follow my lead, and when you feel someone move, move with them. The lissur are predictable. I know their minds better than they do. But don't try to kill one yourself. They're too big. If we can discourage them, they may just look for an easier meal somewhere else." The men started to look more at ease. "You hit any piece that gets close enough. Don't attack the body, you'll only tire yourself out."

In a garden of vortexes all around us, the wet turf crumbled away and the scent of fresh decay filled our nostrils. The first lissurs appeared. They bent their heads slightly and their tips blossomed open, allowing tendrils to spill out like mounds of spaghetti. They slithered forward on the air, reaching for us, but our frantic swings kept them at bay. Two dove back under the surface, and I stepped sideways. The men responded nicely to my pull until we were engaged in a type of dance, drifting as one synchronous entity rather than several.

The ground we'd just stepped from disappeared into a gaping maw and a full-grown Quintha rose from the hole, tipped itself over, and retched the soil from its gullet. It shook its head like a dog and strands of muddied saliva whipped to either side of the huge beast. The tip caught me in the leg and its spur gashed my knee. My blood spilled everywhere. The other lissurs retreated underground and the Quintha followed. The thumping ceased and the ground settled, but somewhere far below, a rumble still echoed.

"No moves," I said meekly, clutching at the fresh wound on my leg.

Time passed. First Ackerman whimpered and broke down into a crying fit, then Cubb began to shriek uncontrollably.

"Quiet!" Lady Malic snapped. She looked at them, her lips in that familiar pursed position. "And you dare call yourselves men."

We tried to corral the boy, but he could bear no more. He fled the circle and sploshed across the clearing. Owen gave chase. I watched in horror as the two figures sprinted through the mist, growing smaller and smaller until they vanished into a milky darkness. I kept listening. Listening. Listening for their demise.

A hungry silence ensued and the men's gazes fell on me for answers. I was about to speak when another leapt from our ranks and ran off to fade into the nothingness of fog.

"Don't be fools," I told them. "You won't survive!"

Then another.

Another.

And three more.

Were they the fools, or was I?

When the rumbling returned, only the Lady Malic and Chamberlain remained. Chamberlain turned to me. "Why don't we run for it like the rest?"

"I don't know if they'll chase us," I told him.

"They didn't chase any of the others,"

Chamberlain said. "If they're coming back up, let's be gone when they get here."

"If they surface and we aren't here, there's no reason for them to stay," I said. "They'll be on the move, and they're a lot faster than we are. It won't take long for them to catch us." A bolt of pain shot through my knee and I clutched my blood-soaked pant leg again. "I wouldn't make it far anyway."

"Why don't you stay behind, then?" Lady Malic asked. She pulled up her dress and drew a rusty streaker out of the holster strapped to her calf. She pointed it at me.

"You won't need that to keep me here. Look at my leg." I showed her the mangled appendage. "I couldn't outrun *you*, much less one of those things. Does that streaker even work?"

"Sure, probably the last one around here that does. I managed to save a few rounds and keep the juice in them active."

"If you think that'll stop a lissur, you're wrong."

"Oh, I know it won't. It's not meant for them," she said. "It's meant for you--to keep you behaved long enough to listen to me."

Chamberlain furrowed his brow. "Excuse me, ma'am, but why are you doing this? He's helping us."

"And he can help us more just by staying put," she said. "We're not cut out for this fight, Chamberlain. You're just an archer, and I'm not even that. We don't stand a snowflake's chance against one of those dirt dragons." She shook the streaker's barrel at me. "But he does."

Chamberlain looked hesitant. I could almost hear his loyalty chip kicking in.

"Come now, it's not as if we're stranding him here. He's armed and he knows these creatures—he said so himself. The Meatman will keep them tied up long enough for us to get out."

"And why the hell would I do that?" I asked.

"Because I can keep Nessa safe. I'll even let her cross over, if that's what you want. But if I die, the boys will eventually get to her. And without my guidance their behavior can sometimes be so… how should I put it… *distasteful*."

Then she took her finger off the trigger and handed me the streaker. I stood agog clutching the weapon.

"On my word, no harm will come to her," she said. "Just stay here and keep those things occupied."

Thump. Thump. Thump. Time was short, and people were harder to read than monsters. I made my decision.

"All right. Both of you, go now." I handed the gun back to her. "Take this—you might need it to keep your word. I wouldn't know what to do with it anyway."

"Feel free to make it out of here alive, Meatman," Lady Malic said. "Then at least you'll know I kept my promise."

"I intend to," I told her.

Chamberlain knelt to lift the woman again, but she waved him off. "My legs are strong enough," she told him.

He turned to me. "Don't think too harshly of our Cardinal. She only does what's necessary."

Lady Malic tightened her siltshoes and wagged a finger at me. "Be good bait and Nessa lives, I swear it." She tinkered with the streaker in her hands for a moment. "The thing about bait," she said, "it works much better if you chum the water first." Then, with a slow and deliberate ease, the Lady Malic turned around and fired a shot straight through Chamberlain's gut. His insides spilled out like hot soup and the bowman dropped facedown into the mud, his gaping wound feeding the soil.

I reached for him and screamed.

"I promised I'd never let Eden take him over, and now it never will." She backed away and crossed herself, then inspected the streaker. "I told you it still works. Now, don't take any of this to mean I lack confidence in you, Meatman. Remember, whether she lives or dies is entirely in your able hands. Fight a good fight and I'll see to it she's left free to enter the bush when her time comes. Don't know why you'd want such a thing but I'll swear to it if those are your true wishes."

"They are," I said, getting up from where Chamberlain's body lay.

"Then so be it." She turned and scampered off, her voice still ringing in my ears.

I took several steps forward and readied myself for the impossible trial. Deep, controlled breaths calmed my mind. The rains came again, flooding the field. Lightning sprites flashed in the distance.

The monsters came.

The first group of lissur emerged, their skin a blotchy patchwork. Calicos. They came at me in singles instead of packs. They weren't smart. Chamberlain's corpse attracted some nibblers. It kept them off me, though, so I had to admit the Lady's methods had merit. But one lissur in particular struck me. Its eyes, to be exact. Its ocular ring wasn't white like all the other lissur I'd encountered on Eden. Instead, they were a deep brown. A familiar brown. This couldn't be...

No matter.

The rest soon found me. I counted seven, maybe eight.

Slice, slice, slice.

I'd fought multiples before, but never this many. I could see Nessa's face in my mind's eye. Her old face, soft and bright, the way she'd been. I had to stop thinking about her. I had to forget everything but the lissur. Thought is slow. Action is fast.

Thrust, twist, recoil.

It was getting harder to swing these damn blades. My attacks grew weaker, and my whole body felt like a fresh bruise. Muscles screaming. Every nerve turned on to full. I couldn't stop the pain.

Chop, swipe, chop again, and again, again…again…again.

Blood everywhere. Thick and dark, a gravy of it. It hung from my clothes. It dripped from ringlets of hair and eyelashes.

And then I realized it:

I couldn't stop them.

I couldn't kill them all.

I was only The Meatman.

I dropped my steel into the mud and unfastened my belt. I took off my vest and let it fall, too. My body melted to the ground. It was time to rest. Finally time to give up. Time to sleep.

I looked up at overstuffed clouds and the lavender streaks of lightning escaping them. Thunderclaps filled the sky. I spoke to Eden, "You've won at last," I told it. "You beat me. Now come claim your prize."

I waited for Eden to wrap me in its shimmering skin, to pull me down, far from the rain. The drops splashed hard against my face. Pinned to the dirt by fatigue, by poison, by doubt, I trained my senses on the earmarks of the lissurs' presence: felt for the reverberations, waited for the low, sepulchral hum, sucked in that cool stench of death that heralds them.

There was none of it.

The dragons had forsaken me. Eden doesn't stoop to respond to the whims and wishes of mankind. Breaking me was enough, I suppose.

11

I lifted myself up onto my hands and crawled to my feet. My good leg began to churn once more, dragging the dead one and beating a slow path home over the abandoned redfield. At the edge of the sink, just before the safety of the bushwoods, I found the land scarred and dimpled with cavernous holes. In each were pools of manblood. At the edge of the woods, I spotted a body—or most of one—in a red frock lying against the bole of a tree.

Lady Malic was still alive when I approached, but blood darkened her clothes and streamed from her mouth. "I thought you'd gone and gotten yourself killed. I cursed you for a charlatan," she said to me with a gurgling laugh before her face grew somber again. I told her not to talk, that the time had passed, but she felt the need to. "I was a just woman, wasn't I? Wasn't I right for trying to save us?"

"It doesn't matter what I think of you," I said, bending over her. "Eden was all that matters, and to her you were just the easier meal."

She opened her mouth and took a final quiet breath. The life quickly left her eyes, replaced by something else. Something of Eden crept in and stared back at me. Not quite alive, but not dead either. I stood while the grasses around her body wiggled and reached upward, covering her. Wrapped in a blanket of green and gold, her body was pulled down into the soil. Then she was gone.

Eden *had* chosen to claim a prize on this day, but for reasons unknown, it was not me. It was time to go. The night was getting old, and Nessa was waiting.

As a flush morning sun dried the world out, I dragged myself back across the safe route. With my game leg, the journey seemed endless. Finally, I came over the little ridge and caught sight of the almond blossom tree and my house. Though it felt like I was running, I was barely upright. I reached for the twistwood door, pushed it open, and called her name.

Nothing.

I stumbled to the bedroom.

Empty.

Outside, clumps of soil, still moist to the touch, dotted the floor leading to the chop house. The door was gone, shattered into a thousand slivered fragments on the chop house floor. The huge tub was overturned, my jars smashed, and their rainbow contents spattered across the room. More mud, like breadcrumbs, led me outside. I tracked a pair of footsteps over the furrowed terrain of the yard and into the bushwoods, but lost the trail in the boscage. I searched for any sign of her. There was only the stillness of the trees. I was alone now.

"Don't leave me. I'll do anything!" I screamed. "Take me with you. Claim *me*!"

On a curl of wind, through the filter of the coppice, a sibilating response crept into my ears. *Never*, it said.

My body collapsed onto the grass, and I wept there until there was nothing left inside me to purge. Only then did Eden make its cruel request. I climbed to my feet and sucked in the air. The damp journal was still in my pocket, so I pulled it out along with a nub of lead and began writing. Someone had to leave a record of what happened here, what came before, and what was yet to be.

Now I was ready to fulfill my promise to Eden. "I renounce them." I released the words into the sky loudly. The wind immediately whispered my new purpose.

I took an unsteady breath and put pencil to page again. Tremors overtook my writing hand, and it shook violently as I pressed the dreaded words out onto the paper.

The colony needs me.

I shoved the book back into my pocket and spoke to the skies again, "You have me. I've sworn to do what you ask," I said. "Now for God's sake, bring her back," I pleaded.

This time there was no answer. Eden is patient, so very patient, and as I was reminded, she does not bend to the whims and wishes of man. I would learn to be patient, too.

AFTER THE FALL

12

Chronicle Entry Z9.14.38:

There are no such things as monsters. There are only those pitiable creatures who are compelled into being. And they are only monsters to those who've never been enslaved by their compulsions.

I am happy.

God help me but I am happy again.

The transport yo-yoed to the surface like a pregnant spider. The hulking, fat-bellied thing alighted onto the wet of Eden's ground and buried its skinny legs in the soil, an ocean of timespace in its wake. It dwarfed the bug of a starhopper we came down on a lifetime ago.

The door of the great machine whooshed open and a young couple—man and woman--emerged, immediately swelling their lungs with Eden's ambrosial air.

I kept to the bushwoods, listening to my people.

The woman turned to the man. "Think there's any Alphas left?"

"If they're here, we didn't pick anything up," the man replied. "I doubt they could've made it by themselves for this long."

But I did make it. I made it all these years and now they were finally here to save me. I prayed I wouldn't have to be alone much longer.

The hydraulic legs of the ship exhaled, and the entire bulbous hull squatted into the mud. The couple stepped onto Eden just as thousands of other faces began to fill thousands of other doorways. In the ship's bloated shadow, the man stopped and picked up some soil, pinching it between his thumb and fingers then putting it to his nose. This brought a smile. He dropped the dirt and wiped his hands together as the woman chuckled at him.

"What?"

"Is that how you clean yourself off?" she asked, wiping her hands to mimic him. "Distributing the dirt evenly? That's ridiculous. You're just getting the other hand dirty, too."

The man paused in mock thought. He took her hands into his, twirled the matching wedding band that clung to her finger, pulled her body close, and kissed her. Then he whispered, "You're absolutely right. It makes so much more sense, mathematically speaking, to rub as much of the dirt as I can onto *your* hands."

She playfully yanked her now-soiled hands away and looked out to the thick curtain of dark teal bush. "There's so much out there," she said quietly. "We might never be clean again."

It was my time.

I shambled out from my perch in the bushwoods. My head and face were covered in gray hair, and the shabbiest clothing hung off my bones. I could see their disbelief at the sight of me. But as more of the new arrivals joined us, they accepted the vision of an elderly man—a human being—with eyes still as blue as spring, surviving on Eden. They encircled me.

"Can you understand us?" someone asked.

I nodded.

"You're an Alpha colonist then?" the first woman asked.

I nodded once more.

"We're the Beta group. Gamma arrives in two months." She gave a wide smile and hugged me tightly before her partner admonished her. The touch of another felt surreal after all this time.

"Is there anyone else left from Alpha colony?" she asked, then quickly shook her head. "I'm sorry, this must be a shock. I'm sure you have questions of your own." She flitted back and forth between myself and her crewmembers. "There are supplies and medicines on board and a whole bunch of new neighbors for you."

It had been so long since I'd used my vocal cords that it took some time to awaken the muscles. There was an uncomfortable pause as I opened my mouth to test my voice. A few plaintive moans were all I was capable of.

The woman stopped me. "Give it time, it'll come," she said. "We're not going anywhere, I promise you."

I smiled what I hoped was a genuine-looking smile and rubbed the heartstone necklace that hung down in front of my chest. Someone handed me a pouch of cloudy liquid and as I raised the straw to my lips they squeezed the elixir into my mouth. The taste was foreign and made me cough, but it felt good. I cleared my throat and croaked out the words from the script. "Alpha colony welcomes you to Second Eden, your new home."

I struck me as odd that the Betas eyed me with a superior mien, as one would a crippled child. I didn't hold it against them though. They were the real children. The newest children of Eden.

A path unzipped before me and a tall gentleman strode toward us. Even from a distance, I could see he had shinier bits pinned to his clothes than the rest of the Betas. He seemed to me not a very patient man. That would change.

"I am Fifth Division Major Marius Cory of the Beta colony," he immediately said. He stuck out his hand and I reflexively shook it. "Are there more of you?"

I nodded.

"We can't locate them. Where are they?"

"Close," I said, my voice loosening up now. "Would you like to meet them, Major?"

A collective wave of excitement passed through the Betas. "We would very much," Cory said. "There's so much to show us. We want to know everything about this place."

"You will," I told him as Eden whispered to me its final instructions. I pointed into the darkness of the bush. "Wade into the thicket there and you'll see them on the other side. It won't take long."

"Thank you for sharing this beginning with us," he said with complete earnestness.

I felt the prick of something, a remnant perhaps, of a vestigial emotion, something I didn't think I was capable of feeling anymore. Was it sympathy? I couldn't remember. It quickly passed though.

"No, thank *you*, Major Cory," I said. "Thank you all for coming to our aid. We can always use some new soldiers."

Deep beneath me, Bean swam slowly in the soil, no doubt trying hard to hide his big, new self. But I could feel his faint hum. Eden's whispers were now a chant banging inside my head, and Nessa's sweet voice was an unmistakable note in the cacophony.

Forgive them their excitement, Mother, your children have been so patient.

Major Marius Cory reached up, barked out a command then dropped his arm like the Grand Marshal of a race. Down the line, a hundred other tall gentlemen and gentlewomen wearing shiny bits dropped *their* arms as well and the Betas rushed gleefully into the bush on all sides of the mammoth transport.

I reached inside the folds of my sleeve and handed the Major a ratty, weathered journal.

"What's this?" he asked.

I looked hard into his face. "Read it," I said and patted the mildewed cover. "It might help you better understand."

"Understand what?"

"That we all have a place here on Second Eden."

I turned my back on him and began to walk toward the bush, hoping I'd done enough to be with my Nessa again. I was wading headlong into the dark brush when he called out to me.

"And what exactly is *your* place here, friend?"

I paused only long enough to answer him, "I am the Meatman," I said. "I bring them the meat."

But I can't be certain he heard me, above the screams.

About the Authors

Rick McQuiston is a resident of Warren, Michigan where he enjoys playing drums, horror movies, football, and spending time with family. He is currently employed at Titan Management.

He has over 300 other publications, including *Demonic Visions Vol I, II, III, IV*, two novels, *To See as a God Sees*, and *Where Things Might Walk*, as well as anthology books including *Many Midnights, Chills by Candlelight, Beneath the Moonlight, As Mean as the Night, Cold, Dark Tales, Michigan Madmen, Private Nightmares, Twelve Days of Christmas Horror, Giant Book of Nightmares* and others, which can be found on: Lulu.com, Amazon.com, BarnesandNoble.com.

Visit Many-Midnights.webs.com for more.

K.R. Gentile is an unwilling resident of Asheville, North Carolina and enjoys zeppelins, clockwork minions, warbot A.I.s, and secret volcano bases.

Other works include:

The Tale-Seller's Night (Prologue to The Scorched Earth), August 2010 issue of *Phase 5 Monthly Review*

Lil Red & The Baron (A tale of The Scorched Earth), September 2010 issue of *Phase 5 Monthly Review* and *Phase 5 Annual Review: Short Fictions, Vol. 1*

Drucy's Tale (A tale of The Scorched Earth, November 2010 issue of *Phase 5 Monthly Review* and *Phase 5 Annual Review: Short Fictions, Vol. 1*

 **Christopher L. DelGuercio** is a Resident of upstate New York, where he enjoys spending time in the sunshine with his family, reading, attending film festivals, disc golfing, listening to music with friends, and laughing.

He is a graduate of The State University of New York at Oswego and current faculty member at The Downtown Writers Center of Syracuse as a fiction instructor.

Other publications include *Blood, Blade & Thruster; Chaos Theory: Tales Askew; Fried Fiction; Parade of Phantoms; Quantum Muse; Space Westerns; Kaleidotrope; OG's Speculative Fiction; Forbidden Speculation; and Tabloid Purposes IV.*

He can be contacted at www.cdelguercio.com

Look for these other Phase 5 Publications:

Sheleasoun: Book I of Beneath the Echoes of Memory by Brandy Wayne

Nerve Zero: A Novel of the Log of The Hand of Tyr by Justin S. Robinson

Phase 5 Annual Review, Volume 1: Short Fictions

For more information, visit

www.phase5publishing.com

www.ingramcontent.com/pod-product-compliance
Lightning Source LLC
Chambersburg PA
CBHW071153180726
48291CB00007B/2438